BOOK 2 OF THE NEW A
FOR CHII

Alice Parker

& the Mind

Magician

Nicola Palmer

NICOLA PALMER

Alice Parker and the Mind Magician

Published 1st April 2012

ALICE PARKER & THE MIND MAGICIAN

For Alice, James and Lily

NICOLA PALMER

Chapters

NICOLA PALMER

Chapter 1

New Tricks

Just a few months ago, Alice Parker had been a reasonably normal thirteen-year old; tolerating school because she had to, struggling to hand her homework in on time, and never satisfied with her appearance. Admittedly, she had been slightly unusual; her eyes were a striking shade of green, and her secret hobbies were growing vegetables and playing the harp. But she had never expected to become super-intelligent in a matter of weeks. Or that an enormous pair of insect wings would erupt from her back.

Alice had become a Fully Integrated Winged Person, or Finwip as they called themselves in the underground villages. Strictly speaking, they were descendants of the winged people or 'woodland folk' who had been written about in children's books for centuries. But that was rarely mentioned. These days, they considered themselves a highly developed race that had evolved to conceal their identity in modern society.

It turned out that her brother, Thomas, and her grandad were also Finwips, but they had kept that a secret until after her metamorphosis. Her parents were not, and Grandad had chosen not to tell them about the existence of Finwips. He was certain that their father would be devastated if he knew his children weren't … normal. All Finwips had a special ability, and Alice's was super-intelligence. As well as this she had a few minor gifts: an over-developed sense of smell, communicating with animals, and being able to fly. Very few Finwips had wings large enough to carry their own body weight.

Alice had been waiting impatiently for Thomas's ability to reveal itself. He appeared to be a late developer like Grandad Parker. The Easter holidays had already begun for Thomas, and now he was home from university, it seemed he couldn't wait to show Alice his new tricks.

One evening while they were watching television before their parents got home, Thomas started channel-hopping. Alice knew he did it on purpose because it drove her nuts, but she still couldn't help rising to the bait.

'Stop it!' she shouted. 'Give me that remote! I was watching that, you stinky nerd!'

'Is that the best you can come up with?' he asked with a grin. Thomas continued his game for a few minutes, with Alice thumping him in fury until he was nearly crying with laughter.

'Don't stop!' he snorted. 'Seeing you in a temper is far more entertaining than any television programme!'

Finally, Alice pulled off one of her smelly school socks and stuffed it under his nose.

'That's a dirty trick,' Thomas spluttered, promptly putting an end to her torment. 'Anyway, I haven't got the remote! It's on the table under that magazine.'

Alice glared first at him, then the magazine, as if she suspected that the two of them were plotting against her in an evil master plan. Thomas held his hands in the air in submission. She got up from the sofa, lifted the magazine and sure enough, there was the remote.

'You've bought another one, haven't you? You're a real saddo!' she concluded, rolling up the magazine and thwacking him with it. He could be so immature sometimes. She turned her back on him in annoyance and stared out of the window at the garden. Suddenly, the slatted blind dropped down with a crash.

Alice shrieked and jumped back in fright. 'I suppose you've been messing with this as well,' she accused Thomas. She tugged the cord to pull it back up and continued to look outside.

'Something interesting out there?' he asked, sniggering to himself.

'Yes thanks,' she snapped, watching a pigeon stuff itself with peanuts on the bird table. It was wolfing them down, one after another, not even stopping to ... CRASH!!! The blind hurtled down again, blanking out the view.

'Oh, for the ...' began Alice. Then doubt crept in to her mind. She turned to look at Thomas who was rolling on the sofa with a cushion over his face, desperately trying to stifle a fit of laughter. 'Oh ... great ...,' she moaned, the realisation hitting her. 'It's you, isn't it? I don't believe it! You're controlling things somehow! That's all we need ...' She sat down heavily in her dad's armchair and dragged her fingers through her hair in frustration. Knowing Thomas, this was bound to be the first of many pranks at her expense.

'I don't know what it is, exactly,' began Thomas, putting down the cushion and wiping tears of mirth from his eyes. 'It only started a couple of weeks ago. But it's been so useful at uni, I've been able to watch anything I like on the telly in the common room! My mates can't understand why the channels they want to watch aren't working!'

'You're so mean!' scolded Alice, but couldn't help grinning at the thought of it. She wished she could do things like that at school. 'It must be fun!' she said enviously. 'Trust you to have a really good ability!' She could imagine the Easter holidays being very interesting if he experimented with it - as long as she wasn't on the receiving end.

'I know,' agreed Thomas. 'You still haven't introduced me to Lucinda's older sister. Do you think it would impress Isabella?'

'You'll never find out!' said Alice defiantly. 'We know what would happen if her dad found a Finwip in his house. I'm not sure I want to go to her birthday party myself, if more of her relatives are going to be there. And *I've* still got eight months before I can be sniffed out, as Grandad calls it.'

'After all I've done to cover for your monstrous eating habits, the least you can do is find me a rich girlfriend whose family owns a castle.'

Alice stuck her tongue out as she turned to leave the room.

'Listen, don't tell anyone in the village about this ability yet,' insisted Thomas. 'Just until I work out what I can do with it.'

*

For the last three months or so, since her metamorphosis, Alice had been managing *her* ability and wings admirably. At school she had been trying hard not to draw attention to herself, but, by now, everyone had grown accustomed to their classmate being a genius anyway.

She had been practising her flying in the clearing of the wood, eager to master the technique after her emergency debut at Christmas. At her happiest when she was flying, Alice tried to devote an hour each week to exercising her wings. Up in the air, she felt liberated and empowered; quite literally, on top of the world. These days she was actually rather good at it, and made many a Finwip envious. Her large, Swallowtail butterfly wings were so powerful, she was the strongest flyer the village had seen for decades. As for controlling the emergence of her wings, that had improved too. There had only been one mishap to speak of.

One weekend she went with her parents to visit Thomas in Oxford. On Saturday evening Alice joined him for dinner in college while their mum and dad went to the theatre. This was the first time that Alice had been 'to Hall' and she was in for a surprise.

The students were seated at three long tables which ran the length of the room. Smiling down at them from their oil paintings were the smug faces of distinguished college rectors, past and present, many of whom hiding behind an impressive beard. Not the female rectors, of course. Alice looked around nervously - it was all disturbingly familiar. She had tried to forget about that night at the castle, but now here she was in a similar dining hall, with a black and white tiled floor and the smell of old wood and polish in the air.

These reminders were the last thing Alice needed as she walked through the bustling dining hall. She already felt self-conscious as a guest, not wearing a gown, while all the students were. Her pulse began to race and her cheeks flushed red. She had scarcely sat down when she felt that dreaded burning sensation across her back. Horrified, she grabbed Thomas's arm and leaped to her feet, nearly falling over as she stepped backwards over the long bench seat.

'Alice! What's wrong?' he asked. 'You haven't even tasted the food yet, give it a chance!'

Alice didn't hang around to reply. She raced out of the hall, down the steps and across the quad. A porter rushed out of the lodge and shouted at her to keep off the grass. After hurtling through the door that she knew led to the garden, she charged headlong in to a group of dons on their way to dinner.

'Sorry, professors!' she gasped before veering to the left and dashing into the library. The college library was quite small and few students used it on Saturday evenings. She ran through it and galloped up the narrow wooden stairs. Before she even reached the top, her wings erupted with such force, they tore through her jumper. Fearfully, she looked down, her heart pounding violently. She wondered if anyone else could hear it.

The only student who was sitting downstairs had her back to the stairs, working at her laptop. Nobody had seen. Alice breathed a sigh of relief. Even then, she tried to hide her face with one hand, and scurried to the end of the gallery to hide behind the furthest bookcase. Sinking down on a stool to catch her breath, she squashed her wings flat against the wall. To her annoyance, she didn't have the blue spray with her - it had been so long since this had happened, she stopped carrying it a while ago. Hopefully Thomas would be right behind her. She heard footsteps approaching.

'OH MY GOODNESS, they are to die for! Are you in a production at the Playhouse?' exclaimed an excited voice.

Alice was startled. A friendly-faced, bespectacled student, wearing a green corduroy jacket had suddenly appeared in front of her. Where had he been hiding? The colour drained from her face.

'Um … well … yes. I am,' she mumbled.

'Well! Those wings are incredible. So life-like. It never ceases to amaze me, what these costume departments can come up with. They must be awkward to move around in, though.'

'Yes … they are. I'm still getting used to them,' replied Alice with a nervous smile.

'I see you've found my secret seat. This is a good place to come when you need a bit of peace and quiet. I often sit up here. You look very young to be a student, though.'

'Oh, I'm not. My brother is, though, Thomas Parker.'

'Ah, the mad scientist.'

'I heard that, Ed!' announced Thomas, appearing behind him.

'Your friend was just admiring my costume for the play,' Alice informed him quickly.

'Hideous, isn't it?' said Thomas. Alice glared at him.

'Far from it! I wouldn't mind a pair of those myself!' replied Ed.

'I don't think you'd make a very convincing butterfly,' remarked Thomas. 'But then again, nor does Alice!'

Ed grinned. 'I should get on with my essay,' he said. 'I'll leave you to it. Nice to meet you, Alice.'

'You too.'

As soon as Ed was out of earshot, Thomas let rip. 'Give me strength! I won't be inviting you again after this! What got in to you?' he growled.

'I'm so sorry. Those paintings in the dining hall freaked me out. They reminded me of that night at the castle … and the fire. There are even a few in here, I can't get away from them! What took you so long?'

'One of us had to be practical,' he said, pulling a blue bottle from his pocket.

'Thank you,' muttered Alice. 'Anyway, he didn't suspect a thing. He seemed to think it was quite normal to be sitting in a library with wings!'

'Well, you are in Oxford. Anything goes here.'

Just as well. She'd got away with it – again.

*

While Thomas had been at university, Alice had to be careful how much food and juice she consumed at home; there was no one to share the blame when large quantities disappeared. Finwips required large amounts of fruit, sugar and vegetables. Grandma Parker made sure she did some baking most weekends, which was delivered by Grandad. His 'meals on wheels' joke was wearing a bit thin – he would insist on shouting through the letterbox when he rang the doorbell. Alice saved most of her weekly allowance to buy extra food in the canteen at school, and Rose, the Finwip dinner lady, gave her second helpings when she could. Sometimes Sarah brought fruit or something sweet to school for her, and Seb's mother often sent some cake. They had been really good friends to Alice, and she felt lucky to have them.

Generally, for Alice, Sarah and Seb, things had been going rather well. Seb was improving in maths, thanks to extra tuition from Alice, so for once he wouldn't have to dread the end of term test. He was actually very clever, Alice realised. But unfortunately, he was easily distracted and still preferred playing the fool to concentrating on his work. In spite of his personality, Seb had been a bit of a loner until he became friends with Alice and Sarah – they just hadn't noticed before. Alice had more in common with him than she had imagined.

Fortunately, any comments about him hanging around with girls just bounced off his sense of humour. Lawrence Lovett and Quinton O'Connor were always poking fun at him about that.

'Look at *your* friend,' Seb retorted to Quinton one day. 'Who's got the better deal?'

Quinton glanced sideways at Lawrence, who was exploring the depths of his left nostril with a pencil.

'Oi, you greb! That's my pencil!' Quinton exclaimed in annoyance.

'I know. I wasn't going to use mine, was I?'

'I rest my case,' said Seb.

One of Sarah's poems had been published in the school magazine and she was over the moon. It was about a butterfly, and Mrs Knight had praised Sarah's vivid description of its wings. Alice didn't need to ask where her inspiration came from, and secretly took the credit. Things had been better for her too – the bullying died out when the novelty of her high marks began to wear off. Imogen had been right about that.

Lucinda No-Bottom was happier these days as well. Somehow her father, the infamous Brian Rowbottom, had managed to hold on to the family home as well as Aylesford Castle and the windmill - much to the amazement of Grandad Parker, who insisted 'something wasn't right there.' Leader of the Sinwips, the appropriately-nicknamed enemies of Finwip village, Brian had kidnapped Sebastian's grandfather last year because he could predict numerical results. Just a few months ago, when Theo was rescued, Brian lost his biggest source of income and feared losing everything. Since then, something had turned his fortune around. But what?

Grandad had been busy keeping an eye on Clifton Windmill, Brian's latest purchase, desperate to find out what was going on there. Judging by all the building work, he was convinced it was something major. Even the sails had been restored, but why? They wouldn't be needed, it wasn't a working mill. That place was a mystery waiting to be unravelled – so he kept telling everyone.

Alice and Sarah had remained friends with Lucinda and had enjoyed more riding lessons at her house. She was still hoping to meet Guinevere and like a fool, Alice had promised it would happen in the Easter holidays. Could she really keep a unicorn's horn hidden from a horse-lover? Even for five minutes? Then there was Alice's fear of bumping in to Brian Rowbottom – she hadn't seen him since the ball at the castle and was worried he would find out that she rescued Theo. So far, Alice had never seen Brian at home; he was always working, even at weekends. She was glad about that, even though she had been told that no one actually noticed them escape that night. Due to the fire, the top of the tower had been shrouded in thick smoke, and the guests could only watch the scene unfold from a distance. As for Hugh Rowbottom, his name hadn't been mentioned since. Alice just hoped he didn't know *who* was in the tower when he decided to set fire to it.

Apparently, Brian had been badly shaken up by the fire and so it was unlikely he had ordered Hugh to start it. Kidnapping was one thing, but he certainly didn't want any deaths to deal with. So Daniel, the Finwip who worked at the castle, had informed Alice and the rest of the village. He also told them that the external CCTV cameras saw nothing that night due to fake snow stuck to the lenses. Father Christmas had already partaken in 'one too many' when he tested the snow machine before the party. Grandad thought that was priceless.

'Now do you see? I always said you should leave him a glass of milk with his mince pie instead of sherry!'

'Actually,' said Alice, 'Dad told us he was reliably informed that Santa preferred a single malt whisky. He said we might even get an extra present.'

*

Alice loved Finwip village even more than she did before, and spent as much time as possible there. Sarah had confided in

Alice that she felt she belonged there, even though she wasn't a Fully Integrated Winged Person. She wasn't a winged person at all, but she admitted she was glad Alice was. Otherwise, like any other normal human being, she would never have known that the underground village existed.

Apart from riding the unicorns and eating wonderful food, they often did their homework in the library with the help of some incredible books written by Finwips. Seb endured his maths tuition from Alice here as well – one meaningful look from his grandad at the far end of the room and he didn't dare misbehave. This is how things had progressed in the last few months. But there had been one or two worrying developments as well ...

Chapter 2

Intruder Alert

Imogen had been looking pale and anxious for quite a while, which was beginning to worry some of the villagers. As the Finwip leader, she was usually a calming influence and it took a lot to ruffle her feathers. She had seen a lot in her ninety-two years, after all. But when she sank down onto a sofa in the library one evening, her head in her hands, Alice felt she had to ask what was troubling her.

Thomas signalled to Alice to go and join Imogen, while he and Sarah carried on reading. Alice didn't really know what to say, without sounding as though she was poking her nose in or stating that she thought she looked ill. At thirteen years of age, tact wasn't one of her strong points.

'Imogen,' she began awkwardly, sitting down next to her. 'What's wrong? Is there anything we can do to help?'

Imogen managed a feeble smile. 'This time, I'm not so sure,' she replied. 'But thank you anyway.'

'Please, just try us. You never know!' said Alice, trying to be optimistic.

Imogen sighed. 'You're very kind, Alice. But I didn't want to worry you all. It's the Sinwips,' she said quietly. 'Something's not right, and I'm really concerned.'

Alice wrinkled her brow – this didn't sound good. 'What do you mean?' she asked.

'Well, for years we have kept our distance from each other, as you know, and agreed to live as separate societies. As far as we Finwips are concerned, our differences are irreconcilable.'

'I should think so too. We know just how cruel they can be,' agreed Alice.

'Ah, yes. But sadly, I fear we have only just scratched the surface,' said Imogen, a look of fear creeping in to her eyes.

'Something has changed. Strange things have been arriving through the Finwip letterbox, and no one should be able to see that letterbox apart from us.'

'And animals,' Alice reminded her.

'Well, yes, as you found out. But animals certainly aren't responsible for what has been happening here lately.'

'What sort of things have arrived?' asked Alice, starting to feel nervous.

'I think they're meant to be messages. Or they could be warnings. Mysterious postcards with symbols on them, random objects wrapped in black paper. All meaningless, since we don't know who sent them or what they want. But the most worrying thing occurred on Sunday evening.' Imogen paused and took a deep breath. 'Someone tried to enter the village via the tree lift. A man who wasn't a Finwip, but somehow he could see the letterbox, and even placed his hand inside it.'

'Oh no!' gasped Alice. Her heart sank at the thought of a stranger accessing the village. The greatest fear of any Finwip was being discovered. But particularly for Alice – she was only just settling into a society where she felt accepted and happy.

Thomas and Sarah had overheard and hurried over to them. 'Did he get in?' Sarah asked, horrified.

'No. Fortunately the letterbox recognised an intruder and trapped his hand. It held him fast until he was released with a warning.'

'What sort of warning?' asked Thomas. 'One he won't forget in a hurry, I hope.'

'I didn't ask,' replied Imogen. 'I just sent Jake and Ethan up to deal with him. With strict instructions not to do any serious harm.'

'I didn't know the letterbox could recognise non-Finwips,' said Sarah. 'That's quite scary! Glad I've never tried to put my hand in it!'

'It was designed by a highly-skilled Finwip engineer many years ago,' replied Imogen. 'Remember when I told you about Ruby, Alice? Our village elder who could communicate with animals?'

Alice nodded.

'Well, her husband, Clarence, had the gift of combining engineering with magic. These days our security system is maintained by his daughter, Nona. She has the same ability. We don't see much of her, though – she's usually busy in her workshop tucked away down the corridor here. You should call in and see her, she's a remarkably clever inventor. I think you'll like her.'

Alice was surprised. 'I would like to meet Ruby's daughter,' she said. 'But now, if the invisible letterbox has been discovered, that means someone knows the village is down here, doesn't it? Someone who shouldn't know.'

'I'm afraid so,' said Imogen gravely.

'Wow. This is quite a blow,' said Thomas. 'The safety of the whole village has been compromised.'

'What can we do?' asked Alice anxiously, hoping that this time the responsibility wouldn't fall on her shoulders.

'I honestly don't know,' sighed Imogen. 'This is a new development with the Sinwips. We've never wanted conflict or confrontation – it's of no benefit to either side. I know that Brian had Theo kidnapped to exploit his ability, but this is different. There's no reason for it, and it's not Brian's style, posting things and literally turning up on the doorstep.'

'Do you have any idea who it was?' asked Thomas.

'No. Jake and Ethan didn't recognise him. They just said he was a young man who seemed rather edgy and angry. It was dark and they couldn't sense that he was a Sinwip, but his metamorphosis could be recent. He must be one, though: no normal human could see that letterbox.'

'No Sinwip could see it either, until now,' added Thomas gloomily. 'I can't imagine who the intruder could have been.

What would cause Sinwips to change, all of a sudden? Why, after all these years, has our security system only just become visible to one of them?'

Imogen shrugged her shoulders. 'That's assuming it *is* only one of them who knows about it. And if so, who?'

Alice remained silent. She already had her suspicions and was devastated that her beloved village might be in danger. Again. She glanced at Sarah, who looked as though she could burst into tears.

'Well,' said Sarah quietly, 'I may not be a Finwip, but I'm really shocked by this. I love this village. There must be something we can do to protect it, Imogen.'

'Thank you, Sarah. But I recommend that we simply wait and see what happens next. And be vigilant. That's all we can do for now. Be very careful above ground, won't you? Especially you, Alice.'

Alice cringed. She felt rather nauseous, convinced it must be someone sent by Brian Rowbottom, wanting revenge for Theo's escape. Someone like Hugh Rowbottom. That sinister beak mask was still haunting her, and often flashed into her mind when she closed her eyes to go to sleep.

'Don't worry Alice,' Thomas reassured her, noticing that she was fiddling nervously with her Finwip bracelet. 'We'll put a stop to it, I guarantee.'

Imogen thanked them for their time, and they headed off down the corridor with worried faces.

'Shall we visit Nona, just to say hello?' suggested Thomas.

'Let's make it quick, then,' replied Alice. They had to make sure they were back home in time for Sarah's mother to collect her.

They found the door marked 'WORKSHOP' and wondered why they hadn't noticed it before. Thomas knocked, and a voice called them in.

'Oh, I know who *you* are!' exclaimed a small lady with long, frizzy, grey hair and half-moon spectacles, as they peered around the door. 'Alice, Thomas and Sarah! I've heard all about you. Welcome, pleased to meet you,' she said, holding out a rather wizened hand with some numbers scribbled on the back of it in ink.

They looked around in wonderment. Her workshop seemed at first like a typical, old-fashioned sitting room, until you spotted the scientific equipment dotted around. Between the books on countless shelves were small monitors showing graphs and red lights, which beeped occasionally. On the dining table amongst tea cups and a three-tier cake stand was a collection of conical flasks with electrodes and wires suspended in their liquid contents. These were linked to another monitor, which looked suspiciously like a toaster with a screen on the side.

Alice noticed a tortoiseshell cat lying next to an old radio that was tuned in to a classical station. She was sure the cat's paws were twitching in time to the music. Could a cat really appreciate Mozart? She certainly wasn't going to ask, not with other people in the room. The cat opened one eye and stared at her. Then it began to 'conduct' with its tail. Alice's eyes grew wide. Then she turned away, wondering if she was imagining it. 'Don't be silly,' she whispered to herself.

'We just called in to introduce ourselves, really,' explained Thomas, looking rather embarrassed. 'Sorry, we don't mean to be nosey, it's just that Imogen told us about your work. We didn't know anything about it, until this incident with the letterbox.'

'Mmm, I'm intrigued by this security breach, I must admit,' replied Nona. 'Sit yourselves down, if you can find a seat that isn't covered in my papers.'

Alice sat down in an armchair and continued to observe the cat from a distance.

'Can I ask,' began Thomas, 'how the letterbox can distinguish Finwips from Sinwips, when we're technically the same?'

'You can. But I won't tell you.'

Thomas's face turned red.

'Well … I'll give you a hint,' Nona continued. 'There are slight differences in our brains, and the letterbox knows that.'

'Can the letterbox scan brains? I don't see how, when you only put your hand inside it. That is confusing.' Nona didn't reply and so Thomas continued. 'What are you working on now?'

'Oh, still the longevity water. It's a long-term project of mine,' said Nona.

Alice turned her attention to the electrodes in water, which were emitting a few bubbles. 'Has Imogen had some of your special water, then?' she asked.

'No!' laughed Nona. 'She doesn't need it. But that is how my research into this began. I carried out some tests on her when we first realised that she wasn't ageing normally. My results encouraged me to try and reproduce what she has.' She glanced at Thomas, as if warning him it would be pointless to ask what that was.

A large fish tank sitting on a chest of drawers had caught Alice's eye, and she wandered over to it. There were only two goldfish in there, but what they were doing was unbelievable.

'Ah, I see you've found Arthur and Phyllis!' said Nona. 'They were my parents' goldfish. They're sixty-five years old now.'

Alice, Sarah and Thomas all looked at her, dumbfounded.

'The longevity water certainly works,' she continued. 'But I'm not going to call it the elixir of life! It has the unfortunate side-effect of humanizing non-humans. When my parents died, I tried to preserve their pets by filling their aquarium with this water. But, while it halted their ageing process, it augmented their brains and they became very bored. I had to make this aquarium from non-reflective glass so that they can see out. They like to read and watch television, you see.'

The four of them gathered around to watch Arthur and Phyllis in their bespoke home. Propped up against the glass at each end was an e-book reader – they had one each. Inside the aquarium, the fish appeared to be reading through the glass, head-butting a plastic button when they needed to turn a page.

'Wow!' gasped Alice. 'This is awesome! These fish are as old as our grandma and they're reading books!'

'Yes,' replied Nona. 'I have to keep them entertained. They soon tap on the glass if they're fed up. Phyllis enjoys a good thriller, while Arthur prefers sci-fi novels. I haven't provided them with a water-proof remote for the TV, though – I think there would be arguments.'

'I've never witnessed anything like it,' said Thomas quietly. 'It beggars belief.'

'Well, to be fair, they were already intelligent. My mother, Ruby, could communicate with all sorts of creatures. Like you, so I've heard, Alice.'

'Oh, I'm not very good at that yet,' maintained Alice modestly. 'What about your cat, Nona? I've noticed that she seems … er … unusual as well.'

'Oh, Mavis is very unusual! I'm afraid she has longevity water in her drinking bowl. Has done for five or six years. She has to live down here now, she was attracting too much attention in my little house above ground. My neighbour saw her sitting in the bay window reading one of my novels one day. What a song and dance she made about it! I tried to tell her Mavis was just playing with the pages, but she wouldn't have it. She saw her put a bookmark in before she jumped down from the window. Her husband was tearing his hair out – he thought Janet needed some treatment. Poor woman, I felt dreadful. So my cat spends all her time here now, as do I, these days. I suppose I should sell my house, really. When I do go out, I leave the television on for Mavis; she likes watching the news or documentaries.'

Alice was thrilled by all this. She had that strange, but increasingly common thought process going on in her mind. Am I really seeing this? Am I really here? Can it really be true? And once again, the answer was yes on all accounts. Like Thomas, she was mightily impressed just how much scientific research could be carried out in a relatively small room with striped wallpaper and a floral three-piece suite.

'Oh, I'm sorry, where are my manners? Would you like a cup of tea, children?' Nona suddenly asked.

'No, thank you,' replied Alice, smiling at hearing Thomas referred to as a child. She wondered if the cups had been used in experiments as well.

'We must go, actually,' said Thomas. 'Perhaps we could visit you another day? I've really enjoyed it. I can't believe all this has been going on and we didn't know!'

'I keep myself to myself, as a rule,' said Nona.

'So, have you tried the longevity water?' asked Sarah.

Alice had been tempted to ask that question. She thought it was quite possible that this eccentric lady could be over a hundred years old.

'No, no, no,' she replied. 'I'm afraid of what the effects might be on a human, having seen what happens to animals. Perhaps I'll feel different in a few years, when I start to feel really old. Then I might be brave enough to test it myself, when I've nothing to lose. At the moment, the village needs me – there's no one else capable of doing my job.'

'There might be,' Alice suggested, staring meaningfully at Thomas. 'He is a scientist, after all.'

Nona looked him up and down. 'I'll think about it,' she said cautiously. 'We'll have to speak again. I'm so glad to have met you all. I shall look forward to your next visit.' With that, she showed them out politely and they heard her lock the door.

The atmosphere was tense as they walked home.

'So,' said Thomas aloud, while deep in thought. 'How does the palm of your right hand reveal the intricacies of your brain? And who could the mutant Sinwip be?'

No one answered.

Even after the excitement of meeting fish who devoured literature, and a cat who took an interest in current affairs and music, Alice was still blaming herself for the security breach. 'I don't know what I'd do without the village now,' she admitted.

'I feel the same way,' said Sarah. 'I love being part of Finwip village. It's so nice having a secret place to go. It's the one thing I have that my sisters can't share. I just wish there was more I could do.'

'Don't worry,' replied Thomas. 'When we think of something, you're bound to be roped in as usual!'

*

Later on, Alice perked up temporarily when she saw what was for dinner. Her dad had collected a Chinese take-away, and anything with pineapple or lemon met with her approval.

'What's the occasion on a week night?' she asked with a smile.

'Well, I figured we can afford a treat now that I don't have to pay for harp lessons!' he replied.

'It would have been money better spent from day one,' professed Thomas. 'We could have eaten at a restaurant every week for a year, for the price of that weird piece of furniture!'

Alice scowled. She had asked her dad to cancel the lessons when she discovered she could play the instrument perfectly well without - one of the perks of her Finwip ability. After two years of lessons, Alice had been average at best; 'long-term intermediate,' as she was politely described by her teacher. Then suddenly, she progressed from intermediate to professional almost overnight. Her mum and teacher were still baffled; her dad was just relieved.

'One expense less, every week!' he grinned.

'Just ignore him, Alice,' said her mum. 'You're a fantastic musician now, so it was worth every penny. Just enjoy the sweet taste of success!'

'I certainly am,' said her father, tucking in. 'For me, success tastes like Kung Po chicken!'

*

The letterbox incident would have preoccupied Alice for days – if it hadn't been for an even more shocking discovery. This one involved Grandad Parker. For as long as Alice could remember, he had recounted vivid dreams and 'déjà vu' experiences. It had always been a family joke, a bit of fun to make conversation at breakfast time – or so she thought. Their grandma had little time for these stories and attributed it to his bad habit of eating chocolate before he went to bed. Now he was actually claiming he had been somewhere in his sleep. Not sleepwalking, but 'dream travelling,' as he called it. He said he had 'travelled' to Clifton Windmill shortly after 11pm on Sunday night, where he had observed a tall man with blonde hair dressed in black.

'He was busy opening boxes, which were laid out on a large table,' explained Grandad. 'Then he touched each individual item inside, keeping his hands in contact with them for a few seconds. Stranger still, he seemed to be talking to himself at the same time. Or he could have been casting a spell, I suppose.'

Alice and Thomas were chuckling while Grandad was telling them.

'You've been watching too many of those cheesy magic shows!' laughed Alice.

'Did you see a white rabbit as well?' asked Thomas.

'You can take the mick all you like,' replied Grandad, irritated. 'I'm telling you I was really there. The large boxes were red with white stars, and the small boxes gave off a green light when he opened them. And I remember distinctly that the young chap had a scar on his chin. I noticed it when he was lighting some fireworks.'

'Fireworks? For his own amusement on a Sunday night?' queried Thomas.

'That windmill is an ideal location, bang in the middle of nowhere,' said Grandad. 'Anyway, these weren't just any old fireworks; he appeared to be testing them, to see if they ...' He stopped himself before he revealed any more. 'That doesn't matter. The main thing is I was there, in one form or another.'

'Oh, John, have you been raiding the sweet jar late at night again?' asked Grandma suspiciously.

'If he has, I'd like to try whatever he found!' said Thomas. 'These dreams sound brilliant!'

To their amusement, Grandad wouldn't let the subject drop until they agreed to test his theory. Thomas suggested that he should travel to their house in his sleep and Alice challenged him to enter her room through a locked door. She would place an unusual object on her desk before she got into bed. If he could tell her what it was the next morning, she would believe him.

Tonight was the night. Thomas insisted on choosing something to put on the desk – something that no one would think of finding in a bedroom. Sniggering to himself at being so clever, he settled on a bag of frozen peas. Alice was impressed.

'Won't he feel an idiot tomorrow?' laughed Thomas.

At ten o'clock Alice locked her bedroom door and turned the light off. Jack settled down next to her in his usual place. These days she was sleeping much better, and dozed off quickly. Just over an hour later, she was woken by the dog growling. The hackles on the back of his neck were standing up and he was baring his teeth. Alice looked at her alarm clock – it was 11.14pm. Oddly, she felt nervous. It was only her grandad, if anything at all. She turned on her lamp just in time to see Jack jump up at her desk and put his paws on it. Suddenly he barked.

'Shhhh!' she whispered. A moment later there was a quiet knock at her door. Alice turned the key and let Thomas in.

'Well? Why did he bark?' he asked.

'I think Grandad's been!' replied Alice, noticing that she had goosebumps. 'Come on, let's phone him now, I can't wait until the morning!' She passed Thomas her mobile. 'You can do it in case he's angry at being woken up.'

Thomas tutted and sat on her bed to make the call. They both put an ear to the phone.

'Ah, I was expecting this!' answered Grandad. 'I hope you're both listening. At 11.14pm by your clock, Alice, I found a bag of 'Captain's Table Frozen Petits Pois' waiting for me on the desk. I had to smile. What an odd choice! Jack nearly made me fill my trousers, though, I forgot he sleeps in your room!'

Thomas threw down the phone as if it had given him an electric shock. Alice shivered. Now they both had goosebumps.

A muffled voice could be heard coming from the phone, which was face down on the bed.

'Hey, you two? Are you still there? Told you so, didn't I? Am I good, or am I good?'

Thomas grabbed the phone. 'Alright, alright, you've proved your point,' he whispered. 'We just haven't got our heads around it yet.'

'Nor have I, truth be told. You can't imagine how annoyed I am, though.'

'Why?' asked Alice.

'Annoyed I didn't realise I could do this when I was younger. Just think what I might have seen!'

Thomas snorted. They could hear their grandma telling him off at the other end.

'We should go,' giggled Alice. 'We don't want to wake Mum and Dad.'

'No, you don't. And I'm exhausted, this dream travel really takes it out of me. We'll speak tomorrow. Sleep well.'

Thomas handed over the phone and stood up to leave. 'Well, there's something that doesn't happen every day!' he whispered. 'And they say oldies don't have any fun!'

Alice chuckled. One thing bothered her, though. Now that they knew Grandad wasn't imagining things, who on earth was that mysterious man he had seen at the windmill? She knew that curiosity would get the better of Thomas, and he would want to find out as soon as possible. Alice was just plain worried: incredible new discoveries in the family, Brian Rowbottom involved in something dodgy ... now *she* had that feeling of déjà vu.

Chapter 3

Weirdo at the Windmill

When Alice awoke the next morning she could hardly believe that what happened last night could be true. Admittedly things were never normal in her family, but this was just *too* strange. *Dream travel*? A step too far. As she sat up in a daze to stroke Jack, she became aware of a tapping sound. There was water running off her desk and dripping into a puddle on the carpet - the peas had defrosted overnight and soaked the books alongside them. Alice groaned as she picked up a very soggy copy of 'Macbeth' and laid it on the radiator. Marvellous. What a great start to the day.

At school, her thoughts were elsewhere. So when Sarah continued to badger her into going to Lucinda's birthday party, she gave in; anything for a quiet morning. Sarah still loved going to the Rowbottoms' house. However, Alice was cautious, and only agreed to go after she had overheard Lucinda complaining to the coven that her father wouldn't be there. Alice didn't feel ready to face him.

'Yay!' exclaimed Sarah, her mission accomplished. Alice grimaced. Sarah's social life was like living the dream; events in Finwip village and invitations to Lucinda's enormous home filled her with excitement. 'You'll enjoy it, you'll see!' she said, being over-optimistic in Alice's opinion. 'Oliver and Damian will be there, you know, Lucinda's cousins who we met at the castle, and she's invited Seb as well.'

'You don't think Hugh will be there, do you?' asked Alice anxiously.

'At a thirteenth birthday party? I doubt he'd want to be there!' replied Sarah. 'You needn't worry about that.'

Alice wasn't convinced. She pictured that creepy character everywhere she went, and couldn't help wondering if Hugh even wore that mask when he went swimming. Was a plague doctor's mask waterproof? 'You realise I won't be able to go swimming?' she said moodily. 'I still haven't found a costume that will cover my wing base mark.'

'Oh no, I didn't think! Sorry,' replied Sarah, pulling a face. 'I'll talk to Freya when we're in the village – perhaps she can alter one for you.'

'Not by tomorrow, she can't,' snapped Alice.

Lucinda maintained that this 'Swim and Supper Birthday Celebration,' as her mother elegantly described it on the invitations, would be nothing special. 'I just thought it would be nice to have a few friends round after school tomorrow. Something to look forward to after the maths test,' she explained. 'I've had enough of grand parties.' Alice couldn't really blame her after the last one.

'Is your dad planning to have parties at the windmill in future?' she asked, unable to resist.

'Probably. Seeing as he's turning it into a restaurant.'

'Wow!' said Alice. 'Sounds like a great idea! A castle and a windmill for parties! You're so lucky.' She thought a bit of flattery wouldn't do any harm. Frankly, unlike Sarah, Alice wasn't bothered where the Rowbottoms held their lavish celebrations.

More importantly, Brian Rowbottom's latest business venture sounded plausible. There was nothing wrong with opening a restaurant, and Alice felt quite relieved to find out that the plan for the windmill was relatively straightforward. At least something made sense today. She didn't tell Sarah or Seb about her grandad's dream travel – she was still struggling to comprehend it herself. Thomas was a bit miffed about it, if he was honest; he thought it put his own ability in the shade. Grandad had asked them to keep it secret for now, even from Imogen. After all, she had enough to worry about at the moment.

*

That afternoon Year 8 were making pizza bases in their home economics lesson. Alice and Sarah were sharing a workstation, while Seb was further down the kitchen muddling through on his own. Alice was aware that he always dreaded classes where they had to work in pairs – he was always the odd one out. But he insisted that she and Sarah continued to work together. When everyone had nearly finished making the dough, apart from Quinton and Lawrence, who were still in a dreadful sticky mess, Seb held his up to show Alice.

'What do you think of this?' he called, pleased with his effort so far.

'Looking good!' she replied with a smile. 'Doesn't smell quite right, though.'

Seb's face fell. 'What do you mean?' he asked her in dismay.

'It smells too sweet.'

Everyone stopped what they were doing and stared at Alice, who had carried on kneading her dough. Julia smiled, remembering the strawberry jam episode last term, when Alice could smell her sandwiches inside the lunchbox in her bag. Katy Smackwell and Olivia Stains-Brown sniggered at the prospect of Alice making a fool of herself again.

'What?' she asked, when she eventually looked up and noticed her classmates' bemused expressions.

'I think everyone's wondering how you can possibly know that from where you're standing, Alice,' said Mrs Brennan.

'Oh, er … well …' Alice could feel her face getting very hot as she stared desperately at Sebastian's workstation. Sarah held her breath and looked even more flustered than Alice.

'Well … he has got a jar of sugar on his table,' Alice pointed out. What's that for?'

'NOOO!' groaned Seb, grabbing the glass jar and staring at the label. 'Why me? I HATE cooking!' He slammed the jar down on the worktop and punched his dough.

'Oh, Sebastian, you've muddled up the containers again, haven't you?' scolded Mrs Brennan. 'Yours will have to be a sweet pizza. You haven't time to start again.' Sebastian raised an eyebrow. That didn't sound too bad.

'Dear me, and you the baker's son!' remarked Lawrence, pointing at him with his rolling pin.

'And what does your mum do?' asked Seb. 'I can tell she's not a dentist.'

Lawrence shut his mouth. He had never been a fan of brushing his teeth, and since he had been wearing a brace, it seemed he had stopped altogether. His smile revealed a flash of yellow rather than white.

'You were lucky there,' whispered Sarah to Alice. 'I think I panicked more than you did! Fancy smelling that from so far away!' She rolled out her dough and laid it on a baking sheet. 'I'm going to call you Alice the Aardvark,' she said with a grin.

Quinton overheard. 'If I become a wizard, will you be my familiar, Alice? I'd like an aardvark.'

'No, I don't think so. We've talked about smells before, Quinton. Yours would be overpowering for any creature. Probably fatal to an animal with a nose like an aardvark.'

Everyone laughed. Even Mrs Brennan had to turn her face away. Hopefully they would forget about this little incident. Alice was angry with herself for slipping up again.

'How do you make a sweet pizza, then?' asked Sebastian, changing the subject.

'You use jam or chocolate spread instead of tomato puree, then you can top it with fruit, nuts and marshmallows,' replied Mrs Brennan. 'Even ice cream and sauce.'

Seb was delighted. 'Now you're talking!' he said. Suddenly everyone looked envious of his mistake.

'Bet you wish you were making a banana pizza, Alice!' said Quinton.

Alice grunted. He was absolutely right.

*

When she arrived home, her grandad's vintage Morris Minor was parked outside. Alice wondered what had happened, he didn't usually call round during the week. As she opened the front door, Jack jumped up to greet her and got his front paws caught in her cookery basket, pulling it to the floor.

'I wouldn't get too excited about today's offering,' she told him grumpily. She found Thomas and Grandad sitting at the kitchen table. 'What's going on?' she asked, opening a cupboard and taking out a packet of biscuits and some chocolate.

Thomas smiled. 'Little pickers wear bigger knickers!' he warned.

Alice cast her most evil scowl in his direction. 'I really don't like you,' she snapped. 'For your information, the only weight I've put on is the weight of my wings. Two kilos is what Imogen says.'

'Nothing to worry about then. Leave her alone, Thomas,' said Grandad. 'We took Jack for a long walk across the fields today, Alice. Around Clifton Windmill.'

'Oh, that reminds me. I wanted to ask you something,' Alice interrupted. 'How come you were back in your bed so quickly last night? Not that you really left your bed, but … you know what I mean.'

'I do. It's strange, but I seem to wake up as soon as I've seen what I need to see. Does that make sense?'

Alice shook her head.

'There's no actual travelling time; I just concentrate on a place, close my eyes, and I'm there. And once I've seen enough, I'm back.'

'Does that mean you can be abroad in seconds as well?' asked Alice.

'Good question! I'm not sure. I'm a bit wary of finding out, though. These local trips wear me out, even though my body doesn't leave my bed. You forget I'm getting on a bit!'

'Anyway,' said Thomas, 'moving on from Grandad's seriously weird ability … Today we actually saw the blonde chap with the scar on his chin. For real. Grandad was right. And it turns out that those red boxes with stars on do contain fireworks.'

Alice rolled her eyes.

'Yes, we watched him from a distance,' said Grandad. 'There was a delivery of those smaller boxes, and he disappeared upstairs with them. When he came back down after an hour or so, there was a green light coming from the boxes. Even in daylight, we could see them glowing. He must have some sort of workshop at the top of the windmill. Then a large crate arrived from a chocolate supplier, which was taken around the back of the building. What do you make of that?' he asked, leaning back in his chair with his arms folded. He seemed very satisfied with their detective work.

'Not a lot,' Alice replied, munching on an apple. 'Lucinda tells me that her dad is turning the windmill into a restaurant, so I'd say a delivery of chocolate is quite normal. And we know the Rowbottoms like their fireworks. I got a bit too close at the castle, remember?'

'Fair enough,' said Grandad. 'But why so many of those … unusual fireworks delivered there? What's the green glow in the boxes? And why does he open all the boxes, lay them out and hold his hands over them?'

'Who knows? Maybe he's checking them over. Maybe he really is a magician. Or maybe he's just a weirdo,' suggested Alice.

'Oh, come on!' said Grandad. 'He may well be an oddball, but something's not right and you know it. I smell a rat.'

'I *saw* a flippin' rat last time I got involved!' replied Alice. 'And I'm going to Lucinda's house tomorrow, so don't cause any trouble!'

'Oh, you changed your mind then! Can I come?' joked Thomas. Alice glared at him.

'Good, I'm glad you're going, Alice,' said Grandad. 'That's useful.'

'Why? There's nothing to investigate, is there? There's a strange man working at the Windmill Restaurant, they've had chocolate and fireworks delivered, and we know that they ordered a cake a few months ago from Sebastian's mum. That's it. Do you really think Brian Rowbottom is stupid enough to risk anything else after last time?'

'It's never a question of stupidity where that man is concerned. It's greed.'

Chapter 4

Looking Death in the Face

On Thursday Alice took cakes to school so they could begin to celebrate Lucinda's birthday at lunch time. But mainly because she realised the night before that she had forgotten to buy her a present. There was one for everyone in her class, though she was tempted to leave out Quinton and Lawrence – they had been giving Sebastian such a hard time for going to a girl's birthday party. Lucinda had explained there would be other boys there but it hadn't made any difference. Lawrence ate his cake very noisily; he had a rotten cold and Alice had already noticed the snail trail on the sleeve of his jumper, where he had been wiping his nose. Quinton sidled over to her.

'Why haven't Lawrence and I been invited to Lucinda's 'Swim and Supper' party?' he asked.

'If I had to guess, I'd say she's worried that the sight of you two in your shorts might put everyone off their food,' she replied. Sarah chuckled.

He turned away looking miffed, and finished his cake. Katy wouldn't touch hers and gave it to Quinton. Her face was easy to read; she was annoyed that she hadn't thought of making cakes for Lucinda herself. Katy and Olivia's jealousy of Alice, since she had made friends with Lucinda, was one thing that hadn't changed in the last few months. Olivia had one bite of a cake, then stopped when she saw Katy glaring at her.

As it happened, there was more junk food to come. Lucinda appeared with a box of eggs wrapped in bright green foil and handed them out. They were large sugar-coated eggs with chocolate inside, then a slightly smaller egg made of orange jelly. Inside that was a third egg that wasn't edible.

'Ooh, what's this?' asked Sarah. 'If you hold it for a few seconds, it lights up! How cool is that?'

'It's called an Egglo,' explained Lucinda. 'Dad's been working on a range of toys. This one's just a trial for Easter.'

Alice watched dubiously as her friends began to hold up their Egglos which were glowing in the palm of their hand. She looked down at her own. It certainly was strange - it seemed to be made of clear plastic, with a swirly pattern through it which emitted a lime green light. That answered one of Grandad's questions at least; the glowing boxes at the windmill must contain these egg lights.

After lunch everyone seemed in high spirits, even though they still had to face their end of term maths test. There had been one or two groans this morning when it was mentioned, but nothing now. Alice had been preparing herself for a sarcastic comment from Quinton, but he said nothing. She thought it odd that Sarah was smiling as she laid her pens out on her desk before the test. Usually she would be in a state of panic by now.

Mrs Myers was running late, and as the class sat waiting for her in Room 12, snorts and giggles were breaking out around the room. Within a few minutes, they were all gossiping amongst themselves. Apart from Alice. No one was talking to her, and she couldn't join in since she didn't know what they were talking about. Even Sebastian stuck his head round the door from his lookout post to say something, which meant he didn't see Mrs Myers approaching. She pushed past him, barged into the room, and gave Year 8 one of her best glares. They didn't have time to stand up as she entered.

'I don't know why you're all looking so happy, considering your performance at the end of last term,' she began.

Katy giggled. Someone whispered something about swords and dungeons.

'Pipe down!' snapped Mrs Myers as she began to hand out the test papers. 'I imagine this will wipe the smile off your faces for the next hour!'

Incredibly, it didn't. Alice felt really uncomfortable; she was being outcast all over again. Just when things had improved. Why wasn't she included in the gossiping? She couldn't believe Sarah and Seb were ignoring her. Looking around, she noticed they were all still grinning as they worked. Alice certainly wasn't, and began to wonder if she was the butt of a large-scale joke. Mrs Myers seemed equally confused and kept giving her an interrogating stare. Alice shrugged her shoulders and carried on writing. She had absolutely no idea what was going on, and some people had stopped working already. Perhaps it was just too difficult for them. She suddenly had an awful thought. Was it something to do with her cupcakes? Had she put too much blue food colouring in the icing? She'd heard frightening reports about the effects of too many E-numbers. No ... it couldn't be. Katy and Olivia hadn't eaten theirs, and they were grinning from ear to ear, doodling in the margin of the page. Maybe it was a sugar overdose from those fancy Easter eggs. That would explain why she felt fine – she could handle plenty of sugar.

When the bell sounded at the end of the lesson, everyone cheered. Mrs Myers remained seated at the front desk and ordered them to hand her their test papers on the way out. Her face was red with annoyance. As she flicked through the tests, Alice, who was last to leave, watched that annoyance turn to fury.

'What's going on, Alice?' she demanded, leaning back in her chair and looking up at the ceiling in despair.

'I wish I knew,' she sighed. 'Whatever it is, I don't seem to be part of it.'

*

Mrs Rowbottom had organised a minibus to collect Lucinda and her friends from school. The noise in there was deafening as they all chattered and laughed. It reminded Alice of when she visited the monkey house at the zoo, only the smell wasn't quite as bad. She didn't bother to join in – they all seemed to be talking about the castle and how much they wanted to go there. Sarah included, and she'd already been. Silly cow. Alice hid her face behind her rucksack and wished she had the courage to open the back door of the bus and jump out when it stopped at the traffic lights. If only she hadn't agreed to come!

When they arrived at the house, Mrs Rowbottom was waiting with the family to greet them. As the electric gates opened, Alice looked nervously at the old lodge by the entrance. Grandad was sure her theory was correct; the lodge did seem to be the entrance to Sinwip village. On Brian Rowbottom's property – how convenient!

Today Brian definitely wasn't there, much to Alice's relief and Lucinda's disappointment. They had drinks in the kitchen area by the indoor pool and wished Lucinda a happy birthday, before being ushered to the changing rooms. Mrs Rowbottom seemed surprised how excited they all seemed, and how talkative, asking questions about the castle. Isabella whispered to her cousins that she was sick of hearing about it. Oliver and Damian agreed. They seemed pleased to see Alice and Sarah, and admitted they were glad there was no dancing involved this time.

'Most of Lucinda's friends are unbearable!' whispered Oliver.

'Oh. Er … thanks. I think!' replied Alice. She introduced them to Seb, who was relieved not to be the only male at the party after all. Although he told Alice he was so impressed with the house, he would have put up with that just to be there.

Alice stared out of the window at the masses of daffodils in the garden, while the rest of the group got changed. A man was taking cuttings from trees and placing them in a plastic bag. He must be their gardener, she assumed. She helped herself to a second glass of orange juice and looked up to admire the patterns in the immense stained glass roof above the swimming pool.

Suddenly, she felt a cold draught and sensed that someone was standing behind her.

'Good afternoon,' said a strangely deep voice. 'I'm Hugh. Hugh Rowbottom.'

Shell-shocked, Alice turned around to find a young man with cropped blonde hair and a scarred chin towering over her. He was wearing black trousers and a black shirt with a silver logo. She froze to the spot. He was no gardener. It was him! The weirdo from the windmill! It *was* Hugh Rowbottom after all! Of course, until now, she'd had no idea what he really looked like. She had only seen him disguised as a plague doctor. If she was honest, his real looks were no more appealing than the beak mask – his nose was horribly pointed. There was something unnerving about his pale, angular face and thin body. How had he crept in so silently? Her stomach began to do somersaults as she stared at him – would he recognise her from the ball?

'I know, you don't have to say anything,' he remarked, looking down at the logo on his pocket. 'Brian can't see the joke – BORE!'

'I'm afraid I don't know what you mean,' said Alice, red-faced, trying to remain calm.

'Brian Oswald Rowbottom Enterprises. To be fair, it was a boring business until I started to change things,' explained Hugh, an evil smile spreading across his face. 'I work for Brian now.' He held out his right hand but Alice was reluctant to shake it, since it was wrapped in a bandage.

'Don't you worry, it's fine now,' he assured her with a skeletal grin. Alice could hear the sarcasm in his voice. In her horror at realising that this could be the same person who tried to access the village, she forgot to introduce herself and shook hands in silence.

'What happened?' she mumbled. She hoped he couldn't hear her brain desperately scratching around for something to say.

'It got trapped in a machine,' he admitted through gritted teeth. 'It was very painful at the time. Lucky I'm left-handed.'

'Yes, it is,' said Alice, wondering if that scar on his chin was the result of his encounter with Jake and Ethan. 'You're Damian and Oliver's cousin, aren't you?'

'That's right. There are three Rowbottom brothers. Senior, I mean. Brian, Patrick and Jeremy. Patrick is my father.'

Although Hugh would never admit it, his father was Brian's long-suffering general dogsbody. Patrick worked his fingers to the bone for BORE but only received a small percentage of the profits. For years he had grudgingly parked his old car alongside Brian's fleet of classic cars, and certainly never wanted his son to work for Brian – he wanted better for him. But when Hugh couldn't get a job after finishing his course in business management, Brian made him an offer he couldn't refuse. He took Hugh under his wing at a very convenient time, and together, they appeared to have turned around Brian's fortune. Hugh was now driving a car worth more than his parents' house, but Patrick still wasn't happy about it. He often looked as though he was sucking on a lemon, he resented his brother so much. Grandad Parker still wasn't convinced that Patrick was a Sinwip. He appeared to have some redeeming qualities.

'I see. No girls in the family?' asked Alice, trying her best to steer the conversation away from herself.

'Not any more,' replied Hugh in a sinister tone. 'Actually, I had an older sister but she passed away. It was a flying accident. She was just learning to fly when it happened.'

Alice nearly choked on a crisp. This was unbelievable! He was so open about their identity and wings! And they'd only just met! 'I'm so sorry to hear that,' she gasped.

'Well, it was tragic, but she knew the risks. You'd never get me into a light aircraft, I don't trust them. Give me an airbus any day.'

Alice felt such an idiot and her red face gave it away. Of course he wouldn't have told her that his sister had wings! She couldn't look him in the eye, but could almost feel his menacing stare through her skin.

He seemed to sense her unease. 'Not swimming today?' he asked.

Alice thought he was rather nosey. 'I don't really feel like it,' she replied. 'Actually, I haven't felt too good this afternoon.' That was no lie, for she had felt excluded and confused. And now this! The day couldn't get much worse.

'Oh dear! Did Lucinda give you one of our eggs? I hope it wasn't that!' said Hugh. Being nice didn't suit him. Alice was getting fed up with his sarcasm, so she decided to continue with the pleasantries herself.

'Yes thanks. I doubt it was that, though. We all had one. They were delicious – do you help make them?' In truth she thought the chocolate was only average and the Egglos a rubbish idea.

'I just add the finishing touches,' he said with a self-satisfied grin. 'I'm far too busy to get involved in the production. I work long hours trying to divide my time between the castle and the Windmill Restaurant. Have you been to the castle?'

Alice panicked – was this a trick question? Did he remember her? She decided to tell the truth. 'Oh, yes, of course,' she replied.

There was a pause as Hugh seemed to be waiting for her to expand on her answer. He had a puzzled expression on his face. Then he took a silver penknife from his pocket. With a swift flick of the wrist he released the blade. Then he hesitated, as if debating what to do with it. Finally he stabbed it into a bowl of olives in a violent manner.

'You should go again,' he said, sounding irritated. 'There's always something new to experience.'

'I suppose so,' said Alice, unnerved by his behaviour. The ice in her drink was clinking against the glass, she was shaking so much. She was grateful when Sarah emerged from the changing rooms and came to join her. Hugh scowled and turned to leave.

'I'll leave you ladies to it,' he said coolly. 'Nice to meet you at last, Alice.'

She may have been on edge, but she knew she hadn't told him her name. Horror-struck, Alice looked him straight in the eye – his were a deep shade of green. He winked at her. He knew exactly who she was, and presumably what she had done. Alice shuddered as she realised she had just met the man who had tried to kill her, Sarah and Theo.

Chapter 5

The Power of the Eggs

That brief encounter ruined the rest of the party for Alice. Hugh was just as terrifying when he wasn't wearing a sinister disguise. Her heart was racing, though not as fast as the thoughts that were flashing through her mind. She was battling with herself to prevent her wings from making an appearance, and could feel the sweat beading on her brow. Sarah and Sebastian noticed that she was very quiet and wasn't eating anything.

'You don't have to continue the act in front of us, silly,' said Sarah, in a low voice. '*We* know you weren't really too ill to swim.'

'What?' muttered Alice with a dazed expression.

'I thought you liked hotdogs?' continued Sarah. 'These are pretty good. They must be posh ones.'

'Actually, I really don't feel very well at the moment,' said Alice quietly. 'I'll be glad when it's time to go.'

'Oh. Oh no,' whispered Sarah, realising that something had really upset Alice.

'Is there anything we can do?' asked Seb, recognising that look of fear in her eyes. 'You did bring the blue bottle with you, didn't you?'

Alice nodded. 'Just don't leave me on my own,' she pleaded.

'We won't, don't worry,' he replied, sitting down next to her with a plate of French fries. Mrs Rowbottom didn't call them chips; it obviously sounded too common. Oliver and Damian wandered over to join them and asked what they had planned for the Easter holidays.

'We won't be doing anything exciting,' moaned Damian. 'Dad's too busy working at the new Windmill Restaurant now.'

'What does he do?' asked Alice.

'He's a chef. He works at the castle as well.'

'Oh! I had no idea!' she exclaimed, surprised and disappointed that he was working for Brian. She wondered if it were possible that their father could be a Sinwip. They seemed too nice. 'You're lucky, having a dad who's a chef!' she added hastily.

'Not when he works for Uncle Brian, we're not,' muttered Oliver. 'He never lets him have any time off.'

As far as Alice was concerned, there was very little to look forward to this school holiday, though in light of recent discoveries, she could guarantee it was going to be eventful. Whether she wanted it to be or not. Thankfully her classmates had calmed down and stopped wittering on about the castle – Oliver and Damian had found it just as tiresome as she had. She told them she had just met their cousin, Hugh.

'Oh, lucky you. At least he's not wearing his plague doctor outfit today! Did he tell you how wonderful he is and offer to show you his Aston Martin?' asked Oliver.

'Er, no, not exactly.'

'Bet he was a moron, though.'

Alice smiled. 'You don't like him, then?'

'We can't stand him,' said Damian. 'He really thinks he's something special.'

'Oh, he's special alright,' added Oliver with a scowl. 'Even his own dad doesn't realise what a nasty piece of work he is. And he's even worse now he's teamed up with Uncle Brian – they're a deadly combination!'

Alice gulped. Did he mean that literally, or was it meant as a joke?

'He's Uncle Brian's golden boy, that's for sure,' continued Damian. 'We were gobsmacked when he bought him that car for his 21st birthday last month.'

'Just gobsmacked?' queried Seb. 'I'd have been sick with envy!'

'We were, really!' laughed Damian. 'I can promise you *I* won't find one outside with a bow on it when I'm twenty-one. We'll be lucky if he sends us a free ticket for the castle!'

'Or one of his stupid chocolate eggs!' said Oliver. 'We haven't even tried one yet.'

'I wouldn't bother,' advised Alice. 'You're not missing much.'

*

She was so relieved when her mum arrived to collect them in the Mini. During the journey, Alice didn't let on what was wrong; she just said she hadn't enjoyed the party very much. Sarah was staying over with her tonight, and Seb seemed annoyed to be dropped off at his house before he had found out what had happened. He knew something had gone badly wrong. As soon as they got home, Alice banged on Thomas's door before charging into her own room and pulling off her blazer. She threw herself face down on her bed and a muffled sob could be heard seconds before her wings erupted. Jack leaped sideways in fright as if a gun had been fired, his tail between his legs. It was only the second time he'd seen Alice's wings, after all.

Even Thomas jumped as he walked in. 'Blimey! I've never seen them burst out so fast! What's happened, Wiglet?' he asked, locking the door and sitting down beside her on the bed.

'I tried so hard not to let that happen at the party,' she sniffled, groping under her pillow for a tissue. 'I've got something awful to tell you.'

Thomas raised his eyebrows at Sarah, who shook her head and looked at him blankly. She must have guessed that Alice's wings were going to break free, and stood well out of the way.

Alice sat up and blew her nose. 'When the others were getting changed at the party, I met the man from the windmill with the scar on his chin.'

'Who?' asked Sarah, knowing nothing about the mysterious man in black.

'Go on,' demanded Thomas.

'It's Hugh Rowbottom. He's definitely a Sinwip, I saw his eyes this time. He recognised me and he knew my name, even though I didn't tell him.' Her eyes welled up again.

'OK,' said Thomas calmly. 'No need to upset yourself. Perhaps Lucinda told him about you.'

'No. He doesn't just know who I am, he knows *what* I am, I'm sure of it. It was him who tried to get into the village – he's got the bandage on his hand to prove it.'

'Ah,' said Thomas with a frown. 'That's interesting.'

Sarah passed Alice the box of tissues. 'I can't believe I missed all this. Was that the blonde guy who left when I appeared?'

Alice nodded. 'It gets worse,' she continued. 'I'm sure he knows I was in the tower when he set fire to it.'

'Oh, come on now, how could he know that?' asked Thomas.

'He works at the castle as well, you see, and he asked if I'd been there. He seemed angry when I didn't say much about it, as if he was waiting for something more.'

Thomas looked puzzled. 'That doesn't make sense, Alice. I think your imagination is working overtime.'

'It is not!' replied Alice defiantly. 'Now I think about it, he was testing me about my wings. He said his sister died when she was learning to fly. He didn't tell me at first that he meant in a plane crash. He wound me up until my face was red and I was panicking.'

Thomas had his head in his hands. 'Well, you're home now, that's the main thing,' he said. 'Is there anything … I don't want to worry you … but is there anything that would

ALICE PARKER & THE MIND MAGICIAN

make you think he was looking for you when he tried to enter the village?' he asked.

Alice reached for her pillow and buried her face in it. She groaned. Thomas clearly had the same suspicion as she did. 'Seriously?' she asked. 'You think that as well? Oh great. I'm dead.'

'Just calm down and think. Is there anything else you can tell me?'

Alice racked her brain, hugging her pillow. 'Oh, there is one other thing. Brian has started making Easter eggs with a strange light inside them. Lucinda brought some to school. Here's my Egglo, look! When you hold it, it glows green. That must be what you and Grandad saw in those boxes – Hugh said he adds the finishing touches to them.'

Thomas took it and examined it carefully. It appeared to contain a lime-coloured liquid in spiral tubing. 'An Egglo, you say? A bit naff if you ask me. It looks like radioactive pee in a plastic egg!'

'I know. But everyone in my class seemed to like them.'

'There's no accounting for taste.'

Sarah was holding her own Egglo in the palm of her hand. She was completely mesmerised, smiling and admiring it from every angle. 'Do you know,' she began with a silly giggle, 'I'd love to go to Aylesford Castle.'

'Oh, change the record,' snapped Alice. 'You've already been! Just because everyone else was bleating on about it today, you don't have to join in. Anyway, you won a family pass, you nit, you can go whenever you like.'

'I'd like to go tomorrow!' Sarah insisted.

'Did she have some booze at that party?' demanded Thomas angrily. 'If you've ...'

'Of course not!' cried Alice. 'There wasn't any! Everyone's been like that this afternoon, wittering on and being stupid. I was the odd one out, as usual. In fact, today's been a really cr …' She was interrupted by Thomas letting out a shout.

'NO WAY! He wouldn't stoop that low, would he? That's appalling, if he has. Seriously clever, though. HE HAS! Unbelievable!' He jumped up and snatched the Egglo from Sarah's hand. 'I'll take that, thank you.'

'Hey!' wailed Sarah. 'That's mine, give it back!'

'Not a chance,' Thomas replied. 'That's not normal light coming from those eggs. It's having the effect of hypnosis, brainwashing people into going to the castle.'

Alice's eyes nearly popped out of their sockets. 'What? You mean … they were all going on about the castle because of those Egglos?' She frowned, thinking back to what had happened at school. 'So that's why everyone was acting strangely! That's awful! I can't believe Brian would do that. But I suppose Hugh would …' She stopped for a moment, trying to get her head around the idea of her classmates being hypnotised by glowing green eggs. Incredible. If it wasn't so wrong, it would be impressive. 'But why didn't it work on us?' she asked, noticing that Thomas wasn't affected by it either.

'As Grandad always says, our bodies are far more complex than those of normal humans. It just doesn't work on Finwips, it would seem. That explains why Scarface was annoyed when you didn't say much about the castle. Unfortunately, having no reaction to the light revealed that you're different, so he probably *was* trying to provoke a response when he mentioned flying.'

'Oh no!' gasped Alice. 'My face will have told him what he wanted to know. How could I have been so stupid?' She banged the back of her head against the wall in frustration. 'Do you think there's still a chance he doesn't know I was in the tower?'

'Only a very slim chance. If he suspects you have wings, he probably assumes that you escaped by flying. I need to let

Imogen and Grandad know what you've found out today. Get rid of your wings and make sure Happy Face here gets some sleep.'

He nodded at Sarah who was still smiling, even without her Egglo. Alice laughed. 'You look even more gormless than usual!' she said. She hoped that Sarah would snap out of it quickly - she didn't fancy explaining to Mrs Wiseman that her daughter had been hypnotised by a glowing egg. Sarah just giggled. When Thomas left, Alice locked her bedroom door and took out her blue spray. A few minutes later she heard him driving off in the Mini to see Grandad. She hoped they wouldn't go spying at the windmill again – it didn't matter how much or how little Hugh knew, she had a very bad feeling about him.

Chapter 6

Crimes at the Castle

The next day, after a lie-in that lasted until lunch time, Thomas went to Aylesford Castle with his grandad to find out what Hugh was really getting up to there.

'This had better be worth it,' he moaned at the kiosk after queuing for half an hour to buy a ticket. When he reached the counter he was furious to learn that they wouldn't grant student discount any more. Realising that the prices had nearly doubled since last year, Grandad paid half towards Thomas's ticket - he still had his OAP annual pass.

'Daylight robbery,' Grandad grumbled. 'No wonder Brian has managed to hold on to this place. First they brainwash people into coming here, then they inflate the prices.'

'My guess is that Hugh is working on commission,' said Thomas. 'Judging by these queues, it won't be long before he can afford a stately home himself.'

'Oh, no,' whispered Grandad, as an elderly lady walked past with a carrier bag. 'They're selling those Egglo Easter eggs in the gift shop. She's bought a few. I wish there was something I could do.'

They sat on a bench for a few minutes, enjoying the sunshine while they ate the sandwiches they had brought with them. They watched a group of castle staff in green uniform gather outside the North Tower, on the far side of the courtyard, chatting happily. Shortly they were joined by Hugh Rowbottom, who handed them each a folder before leading them to the first floor of the tower. They appeared to be trainees having their induction. Thomas and his grandad saw Hugh close the curtains of the room where he had taken them.

'I feel sorry for them already,' said Grandad. 'I bet they're watching a frightfully boring video about health and safety.'

ALICE PARKER & THE MIND MAGICIAN

'Let's hope that's all,' said Thomas.

Half an hour later, the group emerged from the tower and shuffled slowly towards the kitchens. Hugh headed in the opposite direction to the Great Hall. Before Thomas could stop him, Grandad had leaped up and was hurrying over to the trainees. Tutting in annoyance, Thomas followed. They walked a short distance with the two people at the back of the group.

'How's it going?' Grandad asked them in a friendly manner. 'I bet you'll love working here; it's a wonderful place.'

The teenage boy and middle aged woman stared at him blankly. They said nothing, and were now carrying small boxes with their folders.

'What did you do up there?' he carried on undeterred. 'Did you watch a video?'

Thomas elbowed him for asking too many questions.

The lanky teenager with thick glasses broke his stare and blinked several times, as though he had only just stepped into the sunlight. He tried to focus on Grandad's inquisitive face.

'We watched … something …' he said slowly. 'Only … all I can remember is that it was green.' He removed his glasses and wiped the lenses with his sweatshirt. 'I think I must be due an eye test,' he concluded. 'What *was* it about, Val?'

Val said nothing at first. She opened her hand and smiled at an Egglo before returning it to its box. 'It was about our working hours,' she said in a gentle, monotonous voice. 'We shall have one day off for every fifty-six worked. That's very generous, apparently. We get to work at Clifton Windmill as well. We're very fortunate.'

Thomas was aghast. Hugh must have carried out a group brainwashing session on the new recruits. The teenage boy's face was a study. He couldn't believe what he was hearing.

'I only wanted a part-time job!' he moaned, sounding alarmed.

'Listen, son,' said Grandad, gripping his arm. 'I think your glasses have done you a favour today. You've had a lucky escape. Leave right now unless you want to work seven days a week for peanuts. Please!'

He let go of his arm and the boy looked over at Val, who was disappearing into the kitchens.

'I'm afraid he's right, mate. Get out while you still can,' Thomas advised him. The boy looked bewildered. He took off his green cap and stared at the castle emblem on it in disappointment.

'I will then. I don't know what's going on here - and I don't think I want to. Thanks for the advice,' he said, before shaking Grandad's hand and striding towards the gatehouse.

'Throw that box in the bin on your way out!' called Grandad. He leaned against the wall and mopped his brow. 'Poor kid,' he said. 'I'm getting too old for all this excitement. At least we've done one good deed today, though.'

'I'll go and get us a coffee,' said Thomas. 'Wait here. And behave yourself! You can't help them all. Not today, anyway.' As he walked over to a drinks stall, he saw two waiters struggling to carry an enormous tray up the steps into the Great Hall. It was laden with desserts, a large domed platter and a bottle of champagne in a silver ice bucket. Hugh was looking out of the window and checked his watch as it arrived.

Thomas could feel his blood boiling. 'Unbelievable!' he said out loud. 'All these people slaving away so that he can live like a king!' He waited until the staff had gone, then slipped up the steps and into the Great Hall. Hugh was alone at the far end of the room, sitting at the head of the central table. He lifted the lid off the platter, turned his nose up, and reached for the champagne instead. Thomas hid behind the stuffed black bear just inside the door. He heard someone lock it behind him – they must close that room to visitors just for Hugh to have his lunch. With his napkin tucked in his black shirt, Hugh feasted on smoked salmon followed by strawberry pavlova and chocolates, washed down by the entire bottle of champagne. When he had finished, he looked around the room at the same swords and suits of armour that Alice had admired at Christmas, his finger up his nose. Finally he pushed back his chair and let out a large belch that echoed round the room. Thomas couldn't hold his temper any longer. His gaze rested on the knight mounted on an artificial horse. He closed his eyes and concentrated as hard as he could, still crouching behind the rather smelly old bear.

A loud, metallic clatter made Hugh jump. He looked up nervously at the swords and axes displayed on the wall above him. An eerie groan was followed by a grating sound and a heavy thud, as the wooden horse wrenched its hooves free from the plinth. Thomas was rooted to the spot as it stepped down and looked around. He gasped. Did it really just do that? Had he actually seen it blink? He shrunk back behind the bear - he had only meant to make it *move* to frighten Hugh. And frightened he was.

Peeping out, Thomas watched as the horse caught sight of Hugh and turned to face him across the room. Even Thomas shivered when he saw the metal fingers of the knight's gauntlet tighten their grasp of the reins. Him as well? With determination in its eyes, the horse began to charge down the room towards a petrified Hugh, who was hiding behind his chair whimpering. Thomas was flabbergasted. This was too much. He screwed up his face trying to concentrate over the sound of thundering hooves. There was a high-pitched scream, then the noise stopped. So did the horse. Rearing up on its hind legs, its rider wielding his sword in the air, it towered over the table where Hugh had been sitting. It was now completely motionless, its eyes clearly just painted onto wood.

Crouching down, Thomas peered between the bears' legs. Hugh was now hiding under the table, shaking uncontrollably. The door was unlocked from the outside and a security guard ran in, shouting into his radio handset. Thomas took his chance and darted out. He flew down the steps, across the lawn and dived behind the bench where his grandad was waiting. Grandad craned his neck to see him, alarmed that he was struggling to catch his breath.

'Are you alright, lad? What happened to you? You've been gone ages.'

'You really don't want to know,' wheezed Thomas.

Grandad turned around to see countless security staff running from all directions towards the Great Hall. 'Ooh, goody, entertainment!' he announced, rubbing his hands. Thomas peered cautiously over his shoulder.

'Oh no, what have I done?' he whispered.

'Forgotten my flamin' coffee, for a start ...'

*

That evening, Thomas didn't come out of his room - which meant Alice had to go to the supermarket with her dad. He was useless at shopping; even with a list he'd buy the wrong things. She didn't enjoy it either, but couldn't refuse because her mum wasn't feeling well.

Alice took her mum's list and put the items in the trolley as her dad pushed it around the store.

'Blimey!' he said, as the shopping piled up and they headed for the checkout. 'I'm not sure I've brought enough cash! However much will this lot cost?'

Since her metamorphosis, Thomas was always telling Alice to make sure her brain was 'in gear' before she opened her mouth. On this occasion, it wasn't. '£162.28,' she replied without thinking.

The trolley stopped. Alice bit her lip as her father gawped at her. She knew by his face that he could tell she wasn't joking, and she began to turn red.

'Exactly?' he asked, taking out his wallet to check how much was in it.

'Um, I think so,' she mumbled. 'I've been adding it up as we went along,' she said. 'Good practice.' She felt such a nit. How could she have been so careless?

'Let's hope you're right,' said her dad with a smile. 'I've got £165 on me. There must be over sixty items here. I'll be impressed if you're on target!' He took the list from her to check they had everything. 'We just need some grapes, then we're done.' He turned the trolley in the wrong direction.

Alice was starving; they hadn't had dinner yet, and she couldn't wait to get out to the car and start eating something. She put her nose in the air and sniffed. 'Second aisle, about half way down on the right-hand side.'

Her dad stopped. 'You take after your grandad,' he said, shaking his head. 'He used to wind me up doing things like that when I was young. When I walked home from school, he'd sometimes be waiting at our gate. He'd say ''You won't eat your dinner if you've had too many of those sherbet lemons from the sweet shop. Your mother won't be happy!'' I swear he could smell them on my breath when I turned the corner. It was spooky.'

Alice grinned. It was a miracle that he'd never suspected anything. Sometimes she felt guilty keeping such a big secret from him. She didn't know how Grandad had managed it all these years.

At the checkout, their bill was exactly what she had said before they added the grapes. Her dad was delighted she was so clever these days. 'I'm so proud,' he began. Then he was distracted by the sight of a small boy who was plodding alongside his mother, staring at an Egglo in his hand. 'There's one of those flamin' eggs!' he exclaimed angrily.

Alice was astonished. 'How … I mean … what do you know about those?' she asked.

'Enough to know they're not good for little ones,' he replied. 'I've had three callouts to children under six this week who were suffering from horrendous headaches, crying all the time. Each one of them had one of those wretched egg lights! I've no proof that there's a link, but I'd put money on it.'

'That's dreadful,' said Alice. It was. She daren't tell him that they were produced by Brian and Hugh Rowbottom. They obviously had no idea of the health risks or long-term effects. And even if they did, they probably wouldn't care.

Chapter 7

A Smashing Time at the Coffee Cauldron

In Finwip village, an important meeting had been arranged for Saturday afternoon to discuss the week's developments. Alice suggested to Sarah that they should relax in the Coffee Cauldron first – the general mood at the meeting was bound to be solemn, and she didn't yet know what had happened at the castle.

Fay was delighted to see them – they hadn't been in for a few weeks. Most Saturday mornings, if the weather was dry, they preferred to ride Guinevere and Kallisto in the wood. The unicorns didn't like wide open spaces, they felt too exposed, but they did lead Alice and Sarah to a beautiful lake on the edge of the woods. They had no idea it existed before, but now they often spent time with the unicorns there. Sometimes Seb came with them, though he just sat down and ate their picnic. Horses and unicorns weren't 'his thing,' which was useful, since Faunus, the third unicorn, didn't allow anyone to ride him. He was the oldest, and with age came grumpiness. Just like Grandad.

However, Faunus was Alice's favourite. She had learned a lot about unicorns, and the older ones were telepathic. This was perfect for Alice; Faunus could understand her and she could understand him. According to him, Seb was afraid of horses. Alice kept that to herself as she knew he would be terribly embarrassed. Faunus had also shared his real age and recounted some of his experiences in the past, which Alice had promised to keep secret. Generally, unicorns were incredibly intelligent. Even the young ones could sense the emotions of those around them, which is why their wings appeared when the Finwips needed them. The Coffee Cauldron just couldn't compete with spending time with these creatures.

But today it was raining heavily, and as Alice paid for their hot chocolates, Fay whispered, 'Tell Imogen I can't make it to the meeting. They won't let me take the afternoon off.' Alice nodded and took the tray. Since no tables were available on the ground floor, they headed upstairs and chose a spot by the window. There was just one man sitting up here, with his back to them.

They chatted for a while and laughed about Seb's pizza, wondering if he'd eaten it. When they had finished their drinks, Alice's stomach growled loudly. 'Maybe we should have had something to eat, after all,' she moaned.

'Mmm, that meeting could go on for ages,' agreed Sarah. 'I'll go and get us something, my treat.'

'Thanks!' said Alice with a grin. As her friend disappeared down the stairs, she wandered over to the charity bookshelves. She could read an entire book by the time Sarah got back. Having chosen an encyclopaedia of gardening, she selected some cutlery before heading back towards the window. As she returned to their table, she stopped in her tracks. The lone man, wearing a long black coat and wide-brimmed black hat, was now sitting in Sarah's seat. He looked up at her and smiled.

'How nice to see you again, Alice.'

The cutlery clattered to the floor as she dropped it in fright. Hugh Rowbottom! And if she wasn't mistaken, that was his plague doctor hat! In a state of panic, Alice tried to tell herself to remain calm this time. What could he do here, anyway? Sarah would be back any time. She took a deep breath, picked up the items off the floor and decided to play it cool from now on. He seemed taken aback when she sat down opposite him, her back to the window.

'To what do I owe the pleasure?' she asked, a slight waver in her voice as she tried to sound confident.

'I hope you don't mind if I speak bluntly,' he began coldly.

'Not at all,' replied Alice, gripping a knife under the table. She didn't know what good it would do. It looked as blunt as a butter knife, but it made her feel better.

'In case you were wondering, I do know that it was you who helped Theo escape. I knew from the moment you arrived at the party that you were one of *them*.'

'How?' demanded Alice.

'I could see it all when I held your hand. You had a lot on your mind that night, didn't you? In those few seconds I saw what you were, what you were planning to do, what your pathetic Finwip village is like, and even how to get into it.'

It suddenly dawned on Alice that he must have been the lord in the long wig, who greeted all the guests at the ball. 'You could read my mind just by touching my hand?' she gasped in horror.

'Just one of my many talents,' he replied with a sickening smile. 'We Sinwips aren't stupid. Besides, I heard young female voices coming from Theo's room when I went to check on him.'

Alice cringed.

'I knew it must have been someone who could fly,' he continued. 'There was no other way out, I made sure of that.'

'So you did,' replied Alice, her fingers turning white around the handle of the knife. At least he didn't appear to know about Guinevere. 'So, what now?' she asked, determined to look brave.

'Well, of course I can't harm a thirteen-year-old girl,' said Hugh, sounding disappointed. 'Even though you are responsible for taking the largest source of my income.'

'Theo didn't belong to you!' exploded Alice.

Hugh ignored that comment. 'But I have been keeping an eye on your dear brother, Thomas,' he continued.

Alice's stomach plummeted into the depths of her bowel.

'I've seen him leaving your charming little house and going to the oak tree. In fact, I thought I'd wait for him in the lift last Sunday, only that wretched letterbox trapped my hand.'

'Yes, I heard about that,' said Alice with a smirk.

'I've seen your mangy dog too,' added Hugh. Alice's face fell.

'I don't care much for animals ... or children, for that matter. So I'm warning you to stop interfering in my business,' he threatened. 'That goes for your grandfather and your long-haired-loser of a brother as well. What he did at the castle yesterday was just ... childish. The Rowbottom empire is under my control now. Brian just doesn't realise it yet. He's losing his grip, the silly old fool.'

'We're not interested in your business or Brian's!' snarled Alice, fury pushing her fear aside. 'We're just looking out for our own people!'

'PEOPLE? Is that what you call them? You haven't got a clue, have you? We younger generations have never been more different to humans. We're a new, superior breed. We'll take over everything soon, you'll see.'

'What do you mean, superior?' asked Alice, confused.

'Bah!' growled Hugh, springing to his feet and thumping the table with both hands. His face was even whiter than usual, he was so angry. He glared down at her menacingly. 'As if I'd share that with you! I've said too much already. You Finwips are a backward race. Just as well, I suppose.'

'Not backward enough to be fooled by a stupid green light.'

Hugh scowled, wishing that looks could kill. 'Such a magnificent specimen of a brain you have, but what do you use it for? Ah, yes, vegetable gardening and playing a musical instrument the size of a wardrobe. What a waste. You really are a strange child.'

'That's rich, coming from a sicko like you.' Alice was livid – personal insults now! He really was despicable. Well, if that's what he wanted. 'You think you know it all, don't you?'

she ranted. 'Funny how no one likes you, not even your own family. I bet Brian only puts up with you because you make him money. That ridiculous car is the closest thing you've got to a friend! And you look like death – you remind me of a vampire!'

Hugh cackled insanely. 'Oh, I'm not after blood; only brains. Still, it would be a shame if blood were spilled, wouldn't it?'

Alice gulped loudly.

'You've seen nothing yet, you horrid little girl!' he said with an evil stare, running his forefinger over the scar on his chin. 'Just you wait.'

With that, he turned up the collar on his coat and swept over to the stairs, pushing roughly past Sarah. 'And you can tell Mrs Spock on the counter down there to keep her nose out as well,' he added.

Alice put her forehead down on the cool marble tabletop. How far would Hugh go? Kidnap, fire, brainwashing … what would he have done to Thomas if the letterbox hadn't prevented him?

Sarah stood open-mouthed with a large blueberry muffin in each hand. 'Was … was that who I think it was?' she stuttered.

Alice let out a groan. With a tearing of fabric and a horrendous crash, her wings burst forth in defiance as she sat hunched over the table, smashing several panes of glass as they unfolded. She ran to the toilets while Sarah stood helplessly looking out of the broken window. There was shouting in the street as shards of glass showered onto the pavement. Someone was running up the stairs.

'What happened?' shrieked Fay, looking all around for Alice.

'Would you believe me if I said I tripped?' asked Sarah sheepishly.

Alice was angry and disappointed. For the last three months, things had been running fairly smoothly. Now all of a sudden, her wings had erupted twice in forty-eight hours. She had thought these episodes were behind her – obviously she was wrong.

Chapter 8

A Meeting of Mysteries

Alice, Sarah and Fay stood by their story at the cafe; that Sarah had tripped and her chair had fallen against the window. With their help, Alice calmed down. Her right wing had been damaged slightly when it smashed the window, but Fay assured her it would heal in no time. She had to throw her coat away, and decided to tell her mother she left it behind and someone took it. Wearing a Coffee Cauldron sweatshirt instead of her own torn clothes, she made it to the meeting in the village just a few minutes late. There were a few puzzled looks when she entered the dining room. Everyone else was wearing their Finwip robes and had their wings out. Seb, who was there with his mum and grandad, just grinned at the girls' embarrassed faces.

'Imogen,' Alice began, 'Fay sends her apologies, but she couldn't get the afternoon off work.' Imogen nodded.

'So you've come as her instead? Where's the bandana?' laughed Thomas. His sister's I'm-in-a-foul-mood scowl told him she didn't find that funny. Then he noticed Sarah's flushed cheeks. 'Oh Alice, what have you done now?' he asked anxiously.

Although they were in a room full of people, she couldn't help but snap at him. 'I was going to ask *you* that question. Hugh Rowbottom tells me you've been misbehaving at the castle.'

Everyone fell silent. All that could be heard was the pea and ham soup bubbling away in the central cauldron. Thomas's cheeks turned crimson as Imogen turned to him with a disappointed expression.

'Well, Thomas? Would you care to enlighten us as to what's going on?' she asked. 'We now know that Hugh

Rowbottom is a Sinwip, and that he tried to access our village. He has also managed to produce a toy with some sort of hypnotic ability. WHY would you want to provoke him?'

'I … I didn't … honestly,' mumbled Thomas, flustered. 'I had no intention of provoking him. It's just that, when we saw what he was doing at the castle, I lost my temper. I only wanted to frighten him a little.'

Fortunately, Imogen didn't interrogate him any further. Even Grandad had been astounded when Thomas eventually explained to him what had happened in the Great Hall.

'So … when you say *we*, I assume you and your grandad went to the castle?' Imogen said disapprovingly.

Alice was quite enjoying watching Thomas squirm. But before he could respond, Grandad chimed in.

'It was my idea,' he insisted. 'I wanted to find out what that young rotter, Hugh, has been up to. And I'm glad we went. I can now tell you all that Hugh Rowbottom is hypnotising the staff at the castle with that same green light, transmitted through a large screen. He's brainwashing them into working 359 days a year for an insulting wage.'

There was a gasp around the table. Ethan banged on it with his fist in anger. 'I knew something was wrong at that castle!' he growled. 'We haven't seen Daniel down here for a while, have we? So I phoned him, and he said he was too busy with work. Anyway, my kids were pestering me to take them to the castle last weekend, and we happened to see him. He looked awful! He said he was exhausted, but he didn't dare stop and talk to us, even for a couple of minutes. So he's obviously not immune to the green light. But then he's not quite the same as the rest of us, is he?'

'No,' replied Grandad. 'I suppose that would explain why he can't be detected as a Finwip.'

'Anyway,' continued Ethan, 'now I know that those wretched Egglos, which were a fiver each, ended up costing me a fortune for a family ticket. And the kids are already asking to go again! I'm going to smash those green lights when I get home!'

'Good. Tell all your friends to do the same,' said Grandad. 'And when did Hugh tell tales on Thomas, Alice?'

Alice sighed loudly. 'This morning, at the Coffee Cauldron,' she replied. 'He must have been waiting to catch me alone upstairs.'

'What did he do?' demanded Thomas.

'He didn't *do* anything. But he said plenty. He can read minds as well as control them – it turns out he was the 'lord' who welcomed everyone to the masquerade ball at the castle.'

Imogen looked staggered. 'Hugh can read minds?' she said incredulously.

'He said that when he took my hand at the party he read my mind; he 'saw' that I was a Finwip, and could 'see' the oak and letterbox. The night he tried to enter the village, he was actually planning to wait for *you* in the lift, Thomas, and punish you for what I did.'

'Oh, marvellous,' groaned Thomas.

'Oh, heck!' exclaimed Theo.

'He was boasting that he's taking over Brian's businesses, though Brian doesn't realise it yet,' continued Alice. 'There was one thing I didn't understand though; he told me that new generation Finwips, or Sinwips, are a superior breed, who could take over everything.'

Everyone looked at each other fearfully. Grandad froze for a moment, then sipped his tea with a dissatisfied look on his face, as if he wished it were something stronger. Imogen was stupefied.

'Well, if that's true, how does Hugh know about this superior breed?' asked Thomas. 'What does he mean, Imogen?'

'I'm afraid I don't know,' she said quietly. 'Can anyone else shed any light on this?'

It seemed everyone was at a loss to explain it. Grandad fidgeted uneasily in his seat, but he too shook his head.

'I can't answer either of your questions, Thomas,' admitted Imogen. 'I wish I could. Did Hugh say anything else?'

Alice hung her head. 'Just a few insults about Finwips.'

'And he called Fay 'Mrs Spock',' added Sarah. Thomas had to conceal his smile.

Imogen held her head in her hands in despair. Her face was pale and anguished. 'If he really can read minds as well as control them, by whatever means he chooses, then the possibilities are endless,' she said. 'We already know Sinwips have no morals, but it seems Hugh Rowbottom has no boundaries. That's what really frightens me – there's no limit to the harm he can do.'

'Could I say something, please,' piped up a timid voice. It was a small man with pointed ears and a ginger beard.

'Of course, Hester,' replied Imogen.

'Well, yesterday evening, Sam and I took a walk through the wood after locking up the unicorns for the night,' he began. Sam, who Alice knew as the 'pixie-looking stable hand,' nodded. 'It was quite dark, but we could see where we were going, and we soon reached the clearing. Anyway, we heard a noise, and looked up to see fireworks in the distance. So we sat down on a bench and watched them for a few minutes.'

'Go on.'

'Well …,' he hesitated. 'These were mighty peculiar fireworks. We realised that they were conveying a message through the coloured lights.'

'What did it say?' demanded Imogen.

'The robot will rule,' replied Sam. 'Whatever that means.'

Imogen was baffled. 'Are you sure?' They nodded. 'Does anyone have a clue what that could mean?'

Everyone around the table looked at each other with blank expressions. Eventually, Grandad nodded reluctantly. 'I've seen these fireworks as well,' he admitted. 'Hugh seemed to be testing them at the windmill. It was a different message, though.'

'What did it say?' asked Alice. 'You didn't tell us.'

'No. I didn't want to worry you at the time, but I suppose it doesn't matter now he's told you himself. The message said 'Alice, I know'.'

Alice's eyes widened.

'Not exactly subtle, this Hugh fellow, is he?' commented Thomas.

'I realise now,' Grandad continued, 'what Hugh was doing when he was holding the fireworks in his hands at the windmill. He must have been transmitting messages into them somehow. That robot message doesn't make sense though. Maybe he made a mistake.'

Imogen frowned at Grandad. 'What were you doing at the windmill, John? You realise if you were caught, you would be putting us all in more danger? That man is ruthless! I'm surprised at you.'

Grandad blushed, which was unusual for him. Alice felt quite sorry for him.

'Well ... I suppose I'll have to tell you, now I've gone and put my foot in it.' He took a deep breath. 'I wasn't *really* there that night, Imogen. I suppose you could say I was there in spirit but not in body.'

'I'm sorry, I don't follow,' Imogen replied, nonplussed. Looking at the faces of everyone else, neither did they.

'I know this sounds ridiculous. Even for an old nutter like me,' said Grandad. 'But I've finally discovered my real ability. It's been there for years, but I've only just understood what it is. It's dream travel.'

Alice and Thomas felt quite proud of him. Seb laughed – but no one else did. 'Seriously?' he asked. 'This has to be the most amazing thing I've ever heard!'

'Deadly serious,' he replied. 'If I think about a place before I fall asleep, within a few seconds of closing my eyes, I'm there. I can see and hear everything, though I don't have much strength because my body isn't with me. I mean, I can move small things, but my dream body isn't physically powerful.'

Thomas snorted when his grandad referred to his 'dream body'. Seb was clearly jealous. Not of the dream body, but of the dream travel.

Sarah looked quite scared. 'Dream travel?' she whispered to Alice. 'I can't begin to understand how that's possible.'

'I'm still struggling,' Alice admitted.

Imogen was staring down at the table, her hands clasped tightly. 'Well. I can honestly say that in the last few minutes, I've begun to feel my age,' she announced. 'I've never heard anything like it: a Sinwip who can read *and* control minds, a Finwip who can travel in his dreams … I really don't know where all this is going to end.'

'One thing's certain,' said Theo. 'This Hugh Rowbottom has got to be stopped. He can't be allowed to continue exploiting people. Controlling the minds of adults and children is wrong. Children are so vulnerable to manipulation – this isn't just mind control, it's mind abuse.'

'I agree,' said Imogen. 'But how can we stop him? He only has to touch something to have an effect upon it.'

'Cut his dirty little hands off,' joked Grandad. Ethan guffawed and patted him on the back.

Imogen pursed her lips in exasperation. 'Any sensible suggestions? Obviously we can't involve the police for the usual reasons.'

'Can't we turn everyone against Brian's business?' suggested Anna. 'I mean, persuade people to boycott his products, the castle and the windmill?'

'I don't see how, my love,' replied Theo. 'Brian's so influential, he's taking over the town buying up all these properties and businesses. He'd soon stamp out any rumours.'

'That's right. And none of us want a visit from his cronies, banging on our door with a big stick,' added Ethan.

Alice raised her hand. 'We need to do something to affect Hugh's concentration,' she began thoughtfully. 'He really has to concentrate hard to read or transmit thoughts. When I think back to that night at the castle, he held my hand for quite a while before he would let go. I just thought he was a bit of a creep in a long wig.'

'And you were right,' grinned Thomas.

'Good starting point,' said Imogen gratefully. 'What would affect him enough to distract him, though – at least as a temporary measure?'

'I know he's easily frightened,' said Thomas with a wicked glint in his eye.

'And he hates me,' added Alice. 'Just talking to me winds him up. He was wild this morning.'

'I'd say he wound you up pretty well, too,' said Sarah. Alice glared at her.

'I'd rather you didn't act on those ideas,' said Imogen dryly. 'You're thinking along the right lines, but I'm not letting you put yourselves in any more danger. We'll have to come up with an alternative. I suggest we leave it there for today, everyone, and put our thinking-caps on over the weekend. Enjoy your lunch.'

'Let's hope we come up with something before he opens the Windmill Restaurant, then,' said Grandad. 'It says in the paper that opening day is on Friday – local businesspeople have been invited for free food and champagne.'

'That's right,' said Anna, Sebastian's mum. 'That's when they want my cake delivered.'

Imogen stood up, looking drained. 'I'm sure we'll all do our best. Take care, all of you. Promise me,' she insisted. Her focus was on Alice, Thomas and Grandad. They nodded.

'You too,' replied Grandad quietly. 'You look like you need a holiday.' It was well-known in the village that Imogen hadn't had a holiday in over thirty years. She claimed she never wanted one and was happy where she was.

Imogen smiled faintly. 'Things aren't quite that bad, yet,' she whispered. 'But almost.'

Chapter 9

Secrets

After the meeting, the usual Saturday afternoon spread was laid on, but with more treats than usual, since Easter was just around the corner. Alice didn't bother to waste time getting changed; she was eager to start on the food. Besides, her wings had already been out today, and she didn't want anyone to see the damage. She headed straight for a chocolate cake, while Thomas munched his way through a couple of homemade hot cross buns. They all noticed that Grandad didn't have much of an appetite, though. They were sitting at the same table, but he seemed oblivious to them, staring into space.

'Are you all right, Grandad?' asked Thomas.

'What? Um, yes, of course,' he mumbled, looking at his watch. 'I'd like to go soon, if you don't mind.'

Sarah's face fell.

'Is there something wrong?' whispered Alice. 'You can tell me.'

Grandad looked at her sincere face and smiled. 'Perhaps … I should tell you all,' he said slowly. 'Finish your food, you three, and we'll move into another room for a bit of privacy.'

Thomas raised an eyebrow. 'What now?' he whispered to Alice. 'Grandad looks quite troubled. It's out of character for him.' Alice shrugged her shoulders.

About ten minutes later, they were sitting around the table in the small meeting room adjoining the dining hall. Grandad locked the door.

'Oh dear, this looks serious,' remarked Thomas.

'It is rather,' said Grandad.

'What's this about then?' asked Alice, getting worried.

'It's about what Hugh told you. About younger generations having superior abilities.'

They all looked at each other. Sarah fidgeted awkwardly, aware that she lacked any special ability. She started to blush.

'You need to hear this as well, Sarah,' said Grandad, noticing her red face. 'Seeing as you have to put up with all this Finwip business!'

She smiled uneasily.

'Here goes,' began Grandad, sitting down on Imogen's chair. 'This is what I suspect Hugh is talking about. And I think I'm partly responsible.' He scratched his beard thoughtfully, wondering where to begin. 'You may find this hard to believe, but many years ago, I was friends with Felix Rowbottom, Brian's father.'

Thomas exhaled loudly. Alice's mouth fell open.

'Before you say anything, Felix was a good man – a Finwip.'

'No way!' Alice interrupted. 'Sorry, carry on.'

'We became friends not long after we got married, before either of us had children. He was a tabloid journalist, and I met him on one of my first real photography jobs. Anyway, I heard a story about some mysterious activity on the south coast; something about lights being seen in caves late at night. We were both young, and eager to progress in our careers, so off we went to Devon one weekend. We stayed in a guesthouse and borrowed a small motorboat. On the Friday night we set off for Arcanum Cove. Although the cove had to be accessed by sea at night, the tide didn't reach the caves. When we arrived, we turned off the engine and waited in the boat until after midnight. Then we saw the lights, bobbing up and down, moving further into the caves. We dragged the boat onto the tiny beach and crept inside – me armed with my best camera and Felix with his notebook, hoping for the scoop of his career.'

Grandad paused and studied the faces of his captivated audience.

'This is intriguing,' said Thomas, leaning forward in anticipation.

'Go on!' insisted Alice. Sarah nodded eagerly.

'Well, nothing could have prepared us for what we found,' said Grandad. 'I'm not sure what we were expecting, but it wasn't that. We discovered a group of winged people having a meeting. But they weren't Finwips.'

'Very strange,' muttered Alice, slightly unnerved. 'Who were they then?'

'I'm still not sure exactly. You couldn't even call them partially integrated. They seemed to be stuck at what I can only describe as a 'half-way' phase; they could retract their wings but they were only about two feet tall. So they couldn't live in normal society as we do. We thought they were a forgotten group, that their development had been delayed, but that certainly wasn't the case. In all other respects, they were more advanced than us.'

'How?' asked Sarah.

'Were they more intelligent?' asked Thomas curiously.

'When we first spotted them in the cave, the whole group suddenly disappeared. Then one of them reappeared, and one by one, they all returned. It turned out one of them could make himself invisible, as well as those around him if necessary. They had the most incredible abilities: one of them could foretell natural events, so they could give warning of disasters. One was skilled in guiding ships, one had acute hearing, another could communicate with animals – like you, Alice. And one could control minds ...'

There was silence as they all cast each other meaningful glances. Now they could see where this story was going.

'What else?' asked Alice, mystified by her grandad's story. She was desperate to hear more about these different winged people, and was already thinking how much she would love to meet them.

'Well, they were all strong flyers, due to their smaller size. And when we explained who we were, and that we meant them no harm, they welcomed us. We sat and talked all night. We warned them that they were in danger because their lights had been noticed. That cave was the entrance to their village, so we suggested that they found an alternative access point. The following night, we met up again. They wanted to hear all about the Finwips and our village. Anyway, when it was time to say goodbye, their leader, Maia, gave us a gift each. They were just pieces of stone – or so we thought. The winged people had a large collection of precious and semi-precious stones, which they believed harnessed some of the powers of nature, and gave power to those who kept them. Maia said that these gifts would bring strength and prosperity to our families in the future. Felix and I didn't attach much importance to it at the time. We just smiled and thanked them, you know.'

'I don't follow,' admitted Alice.

'I think I do,' said Thomas. 'Are you saying, you think those stones could be responsible for our new, superior abilities?'

'That's my theory,' replied grandad.

'You must be joking! It's not that ugly brown rock on your mantelpiece, is it?' asked Alice in disbelief.

'It certainly is. I agree it's nothing to look at, but there must be something about it that attracts children. Your dad spent a lot of time playing with it as a child – and so did you two. I didn't see any harm in it because I didn't believe all that stuff. Now I'm starting to regret it.'

'What about this Felix chap? Is he still alive?' asked Thomas. 'And does he still have his stone?'

'Oh, he's alive and kicking. But I couldn't say if he still has his stone because I haven't seen him for years. He moved away about twenty years ago – all three of his sons were settled here. Felix was so ashamed that Brian became a Sinwip, he couldn't bear to stay near him. Jeremy's OK, he's a normal human, but Patrick – I'm still not sure. I don't think he's a true Sinwip, he's not all bad. But of the three boys, he spent the most time playing with the stone. That, I do remember. Felix had to put it out of reach, in the end.'

'Do you really believe that stone had some sort of power, which Patrick passed on to Hugh?' asked Thomas, sounding sceptical.

'Well, I didn't … until I realised what you and Alice can do. And now Hugh, of course. Then all I could think about was that wretched lump of rock.'

'I suppose anything's possible,' said Alice. 'Perhaps you should try to find out more.'

'I should, really. I just didn't want to rake up the past, where Brian and Patrick are concerned. Felix hasn't seen them for years, and as far as I know, he's never met Hugh. He'll be devastated if I tell him what's going on.'

'I think he has a right to know, before things get any worse. Hugh is his grandson, after all,' said Thomas.

'It's not all bad,' insisted Sarah. 'You two have amazing abilities – it's only the Sinwips who have turned these powers into something bad.'

'That's true,' agreed Grandad. 'But I can't help feeling responsible, even though I didn't give the stone to Felix, and he didn't know that one or two of his sons would become Sinwips. It is my fault we went to Arcanum Cove in the first place, though.'

'So where does Felix live now?' asked Thomas.

'South Devon. Near Arcanum Cove.'

*

Alice had to leave the room to clear her head. Only it didn't quite work out that way. As she wandered through the dining hall in a daze, she spotted Imogen sitting alone in an alcove. She felt she couldn't ignore her, so wandered over to her. For a moment, Alice said nothing, just sat quietly next to her, mulling over everything Grandad had told them.

'Why does everything have to be so complicated?' she said out loud, not sure if she was talking to herself or Imogen.

'I'm afraid that's part of life,' Imogen replied.

'Nothing's ever simple any more. It's my fault Hugh found the village.'

'No, it's not,' insisted Imogen. 'None of us knew he could read your mind. You did what had to be done, for Theo and the good of the village.'

'Well, I may have made friends with Lucinda Rowbottom, but now I've made a far worse enemy. And he doesn't just want me to suffer, does he? He's already controlling hundreds of people through his green light.'

Imogen smiled weakly. 'That's not your fault either, Alice. Those lights are just part of his master plan to make money – nothing to do with you.'

'I just seem to make things worse.'

'Oh, far from it,' Imogen assured her. 'I doubt Sebastian and Anna think that, after you rescued Theo. And your parents must be proud of your achievements at school. Over the last few months, you've handled everything incredibly well.'

'It doesn't feel like it.'

'We all know it's not easy, Alice, being a Finwip and leading two lives. It's how you deal with things that matters. I can't believe you stood up to Hugh Rowbottom this morning! That took guts. You know, I won't be able to do my job here forever. I may not *look* old, but I'm starting to feel it. It needs someone with strength, like you, to lead this village and fight our battles.'

Alice stared back at Imogen. Was she hinting at something?

'Yes, my dear girl. I am hoping that you will take my place, one day. But not yet, don't worry.'

'I couldn't possibly!' blurted out Alice, alarmed.

'Of course you could,' said Imogen calmly. 'You're strong, sensitive and kind. You've already proved that you can put the village before yourself. And Hugh was right; you *are* superior in ability, for whatever reason. As well as strength of mind.'

'Did you have all this planned before my metamorphosis?' she asked, remembering Imogen hovering outside her bedroom window.

'No! I mean, I didn't *know* you would be capable, but I had high hopes for you. Your symptoms were so severe, I guessed you were going to be a special one, as I told you at the time.'

Alice looked down at the floor. She could feel her eyes welling up with tears, but fought them back. This was too much to take on board.

'There's no need to think about it yet,' Imogen reassured her. 'Of course, you won't need to be in the village all the time, like I am. You need to finish your education and get yourself a good career, before you even begin to take on my role. I can show you the ropes and teach you more about the village and its history. Then you can do what you can on a part-time basis, until I bow out gracefully.'

Alice sighed loudly.

'You can do it full-time when you're retired, assuming you want to,' added Imogen. 'If you have a family by then, and they know what you are, you can bring them too.'

It was difficult for Alice to imagine what she would be doing that far into the future. Strangely, Imogen had never mentioned her past. 'Do you have family, Imogen?' she asked.

'Sadly not,' she replied. 'I was married, though, when I was very young. My husband, Harry, was called up for service in the Second World War. And he never returned.' She stared into space as if she were still looking for answers.

'I'm so sorry, I had no idea,' said Alice quietly.

'Of course you didn't. It was a long time ago,' said Imogen. 'He was a good man, and accepted me for who I was.

Finwips fascinated him, so I was very lucky for the short time we were together.'

'So … what did you do before you retired?' asked Alice. 'If I'm not being too nosey.'

'That's alright, you're not. Although … I'd prefer it if you kept this to yourself.' Imogen looked at her solemnly. Alice nodded.

'I worked for the British government,' Imogen whispered. She paused and looked around to make sure no one was in earshot. 'As a spy.'

Alice was shocked to the core; yet thrilled at the same time. She couldn't imagine Imogen as a spy. It would make sense, though. No wonder she was happy to stay underground in the village. After all, she hadn't aged, so could be recognised easily. That would explain why she never wanted to go on holiday, in case she was seen. Suddenly Alice felt as if she was sitting next to a different person.

Imogen noticed her reaction. 'I should add that I never harmed anyone physically, in case you wondered. After Harry died, I did it for the right reasons and I never exploited my ability. In fact, not ageing hasn't done me any favours at all.'

Alice relaxed a little. Of course Imogen wasn't a bad person. 'I won't tell a soul, I promise,' she whispered. She wasn't sure which was worse: what Grandad had told them about the mysterious stones, discovering that Imogen intended her to take her place, or finding out about her secret past. It was horrible being thirteen. On a day like today, she didn't feel adult enough to deal with all these issues, and wished she didn't have to. Other times, she got annoyed if people treated her like a child. Like when Hugh called her 'a little girl'. Life certainly was complicated.

'We all have our secrets,' said Imogen. 'And I would still be honoured if you would take my place, eventually.'

'Not me! I'm not good enough.'

Imogen laughed. 'You're super-intelligent and can be understood by animals. What more could a girl want?'

Alice shrugged her shoulders and sighed. How about an Easter holiday where all she had to think about was chocolate? Or what she'd watch on TV. She wouldn't even get a say in that now that Thomas could control it with his telekinesis.

'OK then. I will,' said Alice bravely. Imogen hugged her in relief. Alice struggled to breathe for a few seconds – she had a strong grip for a woman in her nineties. Sarah and Thomas would be gobsmacked when she told them. But she had no intention of telling them just yet.

Chapter 10

Chaos Reigns

Alice, Thomas and Grandad racked their brains to think of a way to thwart Hugh's plans. Clearly, for money and power he would stop at nothing – brainwashing was just the beginning, Alice knew that. She also knew she was top of his hit-list. He was determined to get revenge for losing Theo.

When they talked things over, Thomas was desperate to use his ability to cause an 'unfortunate' accident; one that would result in Hugh being unable to read or control minds. At least, for a while. But, as Alice reminded him, Thomas was yet to master controlling the force behind the objects he moved, so the consequences could be dire. And he certainly didn't want to face the wrath of Imogen. It was lucky she didn't know about the *real* trip to the windmill, or exactly what he had done at the castle. They still hadn't figured out how he made the knight and horse behave as they did that day. Alice just wished she'd seen it. She couldn't decide if it sounded more exciting or terrifying. Not a word was said about Thomas's ability to anyone else; the revelation of Grandad's latest one had already sent shockwaves through the village. The Finwips didn't need any more disturbing news at the moment.

The only possible idea they came up with was to deprive Hugh of sleep. Their theory was that if he went without sleep for long enough, he would be too tired to concentrate on anything. Alice could find out from Lucinda where he lived, and Grandad could do a spot of dream travelling and keep him awake all night. The reality was, it probably wouldn't work. Grandad would be exhausted long before Hugh. And they might already be too late …

*

At school on Monday morning, Alice found Lucinda sitting in the locker room playing with a new gadget. It must be something interesting, to delay her from going upstairs to her adoring coven. 'What have you got there?' Alice asked.

'It's the latest e-book reader,' she replied, not taking her eyes off the screen. 'I found it on my dad's desk and thought I'd borrow it. He's never at home to ask, anyway. It's really good. Dad says that one day all school books will be replaced by these.'

'Yes, I've heard that as well,' admitted Alice, ashamed at herself for agreeing with something that Brian Rowbottom had said.

'You can play games on here too,' said Lucinda, smiling.

'Sounds great,' muttered Alice. Although she had grown to like Lucinda over the last few months, she couldn't deny that she annoyed her at times. She was sure that Lucinda didn't mean to show off, and usually, Alice ignored it, but she would have loved one of those e-readers, and was hoping for one for her birthday this year. Having dragged everything out of her locker in her struggle to squeeze her art folder in, she encouraged Lucinda to get up. 'Come on, we'll be late for the register if we don't move now.'

Lucinda groaned and reluctantly put the tablet into her bag. Alice shoved her belongings back inside her locker and slammed the door. They made their way up to Room 12, Lucinda still prattling on about her new gadget. If Alice had been blessed with the same ability as Thomas, that reading device would have flown out of Lucinda's bag and wedged itself in her mouth.

It was lucky their names were quite far down the register – they just sat down at their desks in time. Sarah and Seb raised an eyebrow when Alice walked in late with Lucinda. She just rolled her eyes to say 'don't ask'.

The day didn't improve much. Hundreds more Egglos had appeared; it seemed everyone had one now, and Alice, Sarah and Seb couldn't say anything because of Lucinda. She was bound to tell her dad straight away if someone criticised one of his products. The brainwashing was spreading through the school like a rampant disease – in assembly Miss Frownwell lost her temper and shouted because she couldn't make herself heard over all the talking and giggling. Trips to Aylesford Castle were being organised for every year group; the teachers had given in to the deluge of requests from their pupils.

Back in the classroom, Mrs Barnett couldn't resist having a dig at Lucinda about her father not offering a discount for school bookings. Lucinda seemed quite embarrassed when she was told how much the tickets were.

'Oh ... um ... I'll see what I can do,' she mumbled, red-faced.

'I think it's disgraceful,' Mrs Barnett continued, 'charging children and pensioners twenty-five pounds per ticket. I'm amazed that all the reply slips from parents are coming back as acceptances.'

Lucinda hung her head. Alice, Sarah and Seb looked at each other knowingly. Mrs Barnett's children obviously didn't have an Egglo. Those poor parents would probably have paid anything for a bit of peace and quiet ...

*

It didn't bode well when Seb rushed in from outside the classroom door and sat down at his desk. 'This doesn't look good,' he warned everyone. Year 8 was waiting for Mrs Myers to arrive for the maths lesson, but when Seb caught sight of her furious crimson face coming up the stairs, he decided he didn't want to be the first to encounter it.

'She can't have marked our test papers already, can she?' asked Sarah anxiously. 'Do you know, I can't remember much about it.'

'And why do you think that is?' whispered Alice, giving her a kick under the desk.

'Ow! Oh ... no!' her expression turned from worry to sheer panic. 'I bet I've failed!' she whined, as Mrs Myers stormed in and slammed the door behind her. A picture fell off the wall, smashing the glass in the frame.

'LEAVE IT!' she barked. She put her books and bag onto her chair, then perched on the front of the desk with her arms folded, glaring fiercely at the class. Everyone stared down at the floor looking guilty.

'Last term,' she began quietly, though clearly seething with rage, 'one of you got full marks for the test, while the rest of you were quite far behind. THIS TIME, that same person got full marks while the rest of you got precisely ... ZERO!'

There was a gasp around the room. They all looked at each other in horror. How could that be possible? They'd all written something, hadn't they?

'What got into you all last Thursday? You were all acting strangely, giggling during the test. Julia, Sarah – I thought you two were working, but I see that you were drawing castles and horses instead.'

Sarah's face was ashen and her eyes welled up. Alice could tell she was appalled at herself.

Mrs Myers hadn't finished. 'If this was some sort of practical joke – take it from me, it backfired! This mark will be added to your end of term report and drag each of you down by a couple of grades overall. If you won't tell *me* what was going on, then you'll have to explain to your parents.'

Silence. Alice had never seen so many red faces. It was a refreshing change – for once, she was glad she had done well, and she wasn't even blushing. Still, she did feel sorry for her friends; it really wasn't their fault. Sarah was clearly gutted and poor Seb looked devastated after all the extra work he'd been doing. That test had been his opportunity to show what he could do, but the Rowbottoms had ruined it.

'I'll hand back your papers,' Mrs Myers continued. 'But I didn't even bother to get my red pen out. No one answered a single question correctly, apart from Alice. If there had been marks for drawing ability, then some of you would have done rather well. I've never seen so much doodling on a maths test. Personally, I feel insulted – I wasted a whole term with this class. And for what? How badly do these marks reflect on my teaching? If I'm in trouble with Miss Frownwell, I'll send her to you.'

The thought of an interrogation from the headmistress sent a shudder around the room.

'You will spend the rest of this lesson answering the test questions correctly. You can refer to your textbooks if you must. But no talking!' She walked over to Alice's desk. 'I suggest you go to the library and do some reading or homework until break time. Well done, Alice – again.'

Alice smiled and hurried out of the room clutching her test paper and rucksack. All eyes followed her enviously. As she trotted down the main staircase, the harsh reality of the Egglo effect hit her: teachers could be heard shouting in every classroom around the gallery. Clearly, Year 8 wasn't the only class that was under-achieving. A traumatised Mme Péraud was running towards the staffroom in tears. Glancing down the lower corridor, Alice noticed at least twenty giggling pupils standing against the walls, having been ejected from their classes for disruptive behaviour. She was relieved when she finally sat down in the tranquillity of the library. The school was in chaos. And Hugh had warned that she'd seen nothing yet …

Chapter 11

The Arrival of the Rowbots

The following day began on a mysterious note – *with* a mysterious note. Alice and Sarah were sitting in their usual places whispering about yesterday's events, when Mrs Barnett came over and handed Alice a black envelope. 'This was in the register for you, Alice,' she said.

'Oh! Er, thank you,' she mumbled.

'Ooh, is it a love letter?' sniggered Lawrence.

'Yes, it's from Mr Sheldon,' laughed Quinton. Alice stuck her tongue out.

'Actually, it's a fifty pound note for being so clever,' she grinned, peering into the envelope.

Lawrence and Quinton looked amazed.

'Wow, you lucky cow!' Sarah blurted out. Alice said nothing. She lifted the lid of her desk and hunched over inside it while she examined the contents of the envelope. It wasn't money, of course. She didn't know what it was. Or why it had been sent to her. It was a square, black card with a picture of a wheelbarrow on it, drawn in silver ink. When she turned it over, the message simply read, 'Dear Alice … x.'

Her palms felt sweaty and her face was burning. What was it? What was the significance of a wheelbarrow, of all things? Had Hugh sent it? Who else would send something as weird as this? Imogen had mentioned that strange things had been arriving at the village, and this seemed to fit the bill; a mysterious card with a symbol. Alice stuffed the card and its envelope into her pocket and closed her desk.

'Is everything alright, Alice?' asked Mrs Barnett.

'Oh, yes, thank you. It's nothing,' she replied.

'Judging by your face, it's definitely *something*,' whispered Sarah. 'What's up?'

'I think it's Hugh's idea of a joke,' she said. 'It's going in the bin, don't worry.'

Sarah tutted and shook her head. 'What a dirty trick, sending something into school. I suppose he's trying something different to stop you from concentrating, seeing as the Egglos don't work.'

'That's it!' exclaimed Alice. 'That's exactly what he's doing, why didn't I think of that? Well, it won't work. I'm not bothered by his stupid card!'

'Good. At least our class seems to have got bored with the Egglos now,' whispered Sarah. 'I haven't seen one in here this morning. There are loads downstairs, though, I think the whole junior school has discovered them now!'

*

Mrs Knight arrived for their English lesson carrying an enormous box. Sebastian took it from her at the door and put it on the front desk. Everyone was intrigued.

'Well, Year 8,' a frazzled-looking Mrs Knight began. She paused, studying their expectant faces, and seemed pleasantly surprised that they were behaving themselves. 'I have a treat for you today!'

There were a few apprehensive expressions. Was she being sarcastic? Had she set them a test?

'You'll like these,' she continued. 'Langley School is moving with the times. We are going to test e-book readers on juniors and seniors with a view to replacing most of our text books in the future. In the senior school, your class has been chosen to participate in the trial – there's a tablet for each of you in this box, so you can put your books away!'

Now everyone was smiling. Alice was delighted; she wouldn't have to wait until her birthday now! Ha! Lucinda was barely a step ahead this time, with her new toy! And Mrs Knight wouldn't see how tatty her paper copy of 'Macbeth' had become following its encounter with the frozen peas …

Sebastian couldn't wait to help unpack the box, and delved into the polystyrene pieces as if he were playing in snow. Mrs Knight cleared her throat. 'Before we start to use them, I think we should say thank you. These are a gift to the school from Mr Rowbottom, Lucinda's father. Could we have a round of applause please, so that Lucinda can pass on the message?'

Everyone clapped loudly. Apart from Alice and Sarah, who were mortified. That news really took the shine off their new gadgets. Seb, who was still standing at the front, looked as though he had been slapped in the face with a wet fish, but he had to clap because everyone could see him. He looked helplessly at his friends. Alice was so annoyed, she couldn't stop scowling. No wonder Lucinda had found a reading device on Brian's desk yesterday morning. Sarah nudged her.

'Look on the bright side,' she whispered. 'It's a free gift. And it's about time Rowbottom spent his money on a something useful.'

'Mmm,' grunted Alice. 'I suppose so. But why would he bother?'

Sebastian was handing out the devices carefully, an odd expression on his face. When he reached Alice and Sarah, he pointed to something just above the screen, but said nothing. He moved on to the next row of desks.

Seb had noticed the name of the reading device: 'ROWBOT.' Alice felt as though she had been kicked in the ribs – she breathed in sharply and grabbed Sarah's arm. 'The message in the fireworks!' she whispered. 'This must be what it meant.'

The Rowbot itself had a strange appearance; it resembled a knight's helmet. Laying flat on their desks, it was arch-shaped, with a slightly angular screen representing the visor. Sarah said she didn't like it. Everyone else thought it was great. Alice couldn't help but laugh at Sarah's face. It was as if the Rowbot had been designed purposely to remind her of that night at the castle.

'There are games on it as well,' Lucinda informed them.

'So you said,' muttered Alice.

'My favourites are 'Demons in Dungeons' and 'Angry Bears',' Lucinda continued regardless.

With her left elbow on her desk, Alice hid her face behind her hand. She wondered if Thomas could make the bear in the Great Hall behave angrily. If he could make a wooden horse angry …

'I don't think we'll be needing games, thank you,' said Mrs Knight, sounding irritated. Alice wondered if that was because she didn't have her own Rowbot. Perhaps there weren't enough for the teachers to have one as well. Suddenly Alice threw hers down. When she switched it on, a bright green light appeared around the screen.

'Don't look at it!' she hissed at Sarah. Seb turned around and nodded in their direction. Alice saw him put a piece of paper over the screen. She feared the worst. The whole class, and soon the whole school, could be controlled by these Rowbot devices. She wanted to stand up, and scream and shout, but she couldn't. Who would believe her?

After a brief introduction on how to use it, Mrs Knight explained to the class how to locate 'Macbeth' on the reading device, and they found the scene they had reached last lesson. 'We'll carry on reading aloud,' she said. 'Lawrence, would you read the part of Macbeth, please? Sebastian, you will be Banquo, and Quinton, you're Fleance.'

They began to read their roles, hating every moment. Unfortunately, their new Rowbots made no difference to their struggle with Shakespearian language. Seb was reading from his textbook concealed on his lap, to avoid looking at the green light. Alice was just waiting for one of them to mention the castle or start giggling …

Nothing happened. The boys were reading sensibly, Mrs Knight seemed happy. Lawrence began Macbeth's long speech. Then suddenly, Alice's heart nearly stopped at the sound of one word.

'Is this a wheelbarrow which I see before me,
The handle toward my hand?' read Lawrence.

'LAWRENCE!' scolded Mrs Knight. Everyone looked up. 'WHAT did you just say? What does Macbeth actually see before him?'

Lawrence's cheeks began to colour – he looked genuinely confused. 'Er, a wheelbarrow,' he muttered.

Mrs Knight rolled her eyes. 'Very funny. Lydia, what does Macbeth see, please?'

'Um ... well ... a wheelbarrow, Miss,' she said timidly.

Mrs Knight was losing her patience. Slamming down her textbook, she stormed over to Lydia and seized her Rowbot from her hands. 'It says DAGGER!' she growled.

Lucinda put her hand up. 'Mine says wheelbarrow too,' she said. Even she wasn't exempt from her cousin's mind control.

'So does mine.' 'And mine!' 'Mine too!' piped up everyone else.

One by one, Mrs Knight studied all their Rowbots, then returned to the front desk, glowering. 'ALL of your devices say DAGGER!' she roared.

Everyone looked genuinely terrified, and completely baffled. Alice felt sick, her hands were trembling. Sarah noticed.

'This is bad, isn't it?' she whispered. Alice nodded. She realised that the green light could only influence readers if they had been exposed to it for a while. It had no effect on Mrs Knight, as she only glanced at the Rowbots briefly. What she saw was the actual text – not the alterations and messages that had brainwashed most of her class.

'Well, I'm disappointed,' continued Mrs Knight. 'Put your Rowbots away and take out your textbooks. If you can't use them sensibly, we won't use them at all.'

They did as they were told. Lucinda pulled a face. Alice could hardly read Act 2 in her copy, the pages were so damaged after she pulled them apart. But even when the green lights were turned off, and they began reading from their books, the lesson did not continue smoothly. Year 8 began to be silly – the giggling was infectious. It was just like Thursday afternoon, when they had been exposed to the Egglos. Only this time the whispering wasn't about the castle, it was about wheelbarrows. *Wheelbarrows* of all things. Hugh was just making a point, that he could do *anything*. Alice didn't want to look different, so she joined in and nudged Sarah to do the same. Soon Seb followed their example. Mrs Knight was nearly tearing her hair out and shouted until she was hoarse. Everyone was glad when the bell sounded at the end of the lesson.

Sarah and Sebastian were appalled when Alice showed them the wheelbarrow card at break time. They were sitting on a bench in the playground. Sarah had her head in her hands. 'Hugh's playing with our brains,' she said in disgust. 'It's not right. He has to be stopped. My mum and dad will go mad when they see my maths report.'

'Well, at least my grandad will understand the real reason for my result,' said Seb. 'What do you think's been happening with the Rowbots in the junior class this morning?'

'Oh, no, I forgot about that,' exclaimed Alice. She looked around the playground. One class appeared to be missing. 'I can't see the Fourth Years,' she said. A young boy from Year 5 ran past, chasing his football, and Alice took the opportunity to ask him.

'Oh, they're being kept inside during break,' he announced. 'For being naughty in their lesson – we heard their teacher yelling at them!' he added with grin.

'The poor things,' sighed Seb. The three of them spent the rest of break on their bench looking miserable.

*

There was more of the same to come. In science, Mrs Dawkins asked them to copy a diagram from their textbook on the Rowbot, showing the apparatus used to collect a sample of hydrogen. When everyone had been drawing for a few minutes, she took a wander along the front bench. A bemused smile crept over her face – she had a good sense of humour and rarely got angry.

'Lydia, what have you drawn there?' she asked.

Lydia looked up, blushing. 'Oh. It looks like a wheelbarrow, doesn't it? I'll rub it out.'

'How funny!' laughed Mrs Dawkins, continuing along the row. 'Quinton, you've done ... so have you, Lawrence! Are you all copying each other?' she asked, looking confused.

This time, Lydia took the hint and pulled out her textbook. She had noticed that Seb, Sarah and Alice weren't using their Rowbots. Mrs Dawkins didn't go any further than the first bench, so most of the class went home with notes concluding that, *'Hydrogen makes a lighted splint go 'Pop.' A sample can be obtained using the apparatus above.'* A wheelbarrow. Of course.

Sarah went home with Alice after school, as was usual on a Tuesday afternoon. Today, Seb joined them, since his mother was working late to finish a birthday cake. As Alice opened the gate, Thomas and Jack hurried down the steps to meet her.

'This enormous box is for you!' he informed her, pointing to a parcel on the path that was over a metre wide and nearly as tall. 'It came by special delivery this morning, just after you left. What on earth is it? Spill the beans!' he said impatiently.

Alice didn't answer. A chill went down her spine. It was a black cardboard box with silver ribbon. She put her arms around Jack for reassurance, as Thomas began to cut the tape with scissors. 'This is an impressive parcel! Have you got an admirer? Would you rather open it yourself?' he asked.

Alice shook her head. She was reluctant to go near it. Thomas opened the top of the box and peered inside. 'Oh,' he said, looking disappointed. 'Bit of an anti-climax. Sorry folks.'

Seb stepped forward and helped him tear open the side. They pulled out a large silver wheelbarrow. Sarah gasped.

'Predictable,' said Seb. 'But still sick.'

'I'm going to kill him!' snarled Alice, stomping up the steps into the house. Jack ran after her.

'Who? Oh no, what's happened today?' asked Thomas, noticing Sarah and Seb's glum faces.

'We'll fill you in,' replied Seb. 'But you're not going to like it. Hugh's gone too far this time.'

Chapter 12

Nothing is Coincidence

So, 'the robot will rule' message in the fireworks had materialised; as a *Rowbot* that was certainly ruling the minds of many pupils at Langley School. After Seb and Sarah had shown Thomas their Rowbots and tried to explain what had been happening that day, he phoned his grandad straight away. He and Alice needed an excuse to visit him as soon as possible.

Shortly after their mother arrived home, Grandma phoned.

'Thomas, Alice,' their mother called up the stairs. 'Grandma Parker has made a lemon and sultana cheesecake for you. She wants you to collect it this evening, while it's fresh. So do I, it's my favourite! You can take the car, Thomas.'

'OK, will do!' he shouted. 'Excellent,' he said to Alice. 'Our excuse is in place.'

'That cheesecake sounds good!' said Seb. 'Do *we* get a piece tomorrow?'

'Maybe!' laughed Alice, hoping that there really was a cheesecake, at such short notice.

When Sarah and Seb had gone home, Alice and Thomas wolfed down their dinner, keen to get over to their grandparents' house. While they were eating, their mother took the opportunity to ask a question. Their dad was working late.

'When I went shopping yesterday lunch time,' she began, 'I bought two mangos, a large pineapple and two cartons of orange juice. Have you polished them off already, Thomas? My food bill is horrendous these days!'

Alice stared at him, silently urging him to say yes.

He didn't look up. 'It wasn't me,' he replied. 'Must have been Wiglet, here.'

Thomas received a kick on the shin under the table.

'Sorry mum,' said Alice sheepishly. 'They were really nice, though.'

'I'm surprised all that fruit didn't make you ill,' replied her mother, tutting and shaking her head. 'Still, at least it wasn't chocolate.'

Thomas grinned.

'I hate you,' whispered Alice.

Splat. The food on her fork suddenly fell back onto her plate, splattering Alice and the table in gravy.

'Messy child,' said Thomas, shaking his head.

Alice was angry now. He'd done that! How she despised his ability! She wiped the table and carried on eating.

'Can't take you anywhere,' muttered Thomas with a smile.

'Is that what Grandad said when you caused trouble at the castle?' snapped Alice.

'What happened there, then?' asked her mother, frowning.

Thomas scowled. Clunk. Alice's glass of water suddenly fell over, flooding the remaining food on her plate and soaking her jeans.

'STOP IT!' she yelled, jumping up from the table.

'Stop what?' asked Thomas, putting on a surprised face.

'What's got into you two?' demanded their mother. Alice mopped up the water with a cloth and threw it at her brother before storming up to her room. Jack followed her.

'Bad day at school, I expect,' said Thomas. 'Are you going to the opening of the Windmill Restaurant, Mum? I heard the Rowbottoms were inviting local businesspeople.'

'Mmm. Not me, though. I'm quite disappointed. Your dad and I were looking forward to trying Jeremy's cooking – apparently he's a talented chef. Alice must have had some of his food at the ball. Somehow Brian has managed to persuade him to cook at the windmill as well as the castle.'

'Jeremy ... Rowbottom? I didn't know he worked for his Brian as well.'

'Oh, yes. I don't suppose he has much choice – I should imagine his brother is a very forceful man.'

*

Thomas had to grovel and apologise to Alice before she would leave the house with him. She hadn't found his little game at the dinner table remotely funny. She hid her Rowbot inside her coat to show her grandad.

He was just parking his car when they arrived. 'I had to dash out to get bloomin' cream cheese and lemons!' he complained. 'You can't go home empty-handed, your mum's expecting a cheesecake!'

Grandma was pleased to see them, even though she would be stuck in the kitchen. 'I've heard one or two things from your grandad about what's going on,' she said, looking worried. 'I don't like the sound of it one bit. I hope you can come up with a way to put a stop to it all.'

'So do I,' replied Thomas. 'But I don't think it will be easy.'

Grandad made them a hot chocolate and they sat down at the table. Alice took out her Rowbot and handed it to her grandad.

'Ah, this is the offending article,' he said, switching it on to see the green light. 'Well, I'm not exactly surprised, but I am disgusted. I never thought Brian would stoop low enough to target children. It must be the influence of this Hugh character.'

'School is just awful at the moment,' moaned Alice. 'There's so much confusion, and people acting strangely. Only two classes have been given Rowbots. And Miss Frownwell, of course, though hers looks a bit different. But most of the other kids have got an Egglo. So if they're not being shouted at in lessons for getting things wrong, they're being silly and asking to go to the castle. There are trips being organised for every class.'

'Brian must be rubbing his hands,' replied Grandad disdainfully. 'The bad news is, he hasn't only given them to your school. There's an article in today's paper which says B.O.R.E. has provided a dozen schools in the area with Rowbot reading devices. Brian invited the head teachers to dinner at the castle to launch this project of his, and the evening ended with ... surprise, surprise ... a firework display!'

'Oh, for pity's sake!' gasped Alice. 'It gets worse! What's the good news?'

'Well, the Rowbots aren't having a serious effect – for the moment, at least. I mean, Hugh just seems to be testing them, having a bit of fun while he decides what to do with them.'

'What do you mean?' asked Alice, chasing the marshmallows in her drink with a teaspoon.

'So far, it's just a daft prank, isn't it, winding up the children and teachers? But any day now, the real purpose of the Rowbots will become apparent.'

Alice's face fell. 'And what's that?' she asked. 'Do you know?'

'I think I do. I'm afraid I went to Clifton Windmill again last night,' replied Grandad. 'You know, by dream travel. Extremely interesting it was too, I couldn't have timed it better. Brian and Hugh were having a very late meeting in the wine cellar. I'd love a cellar like that, it's huge!'

'Oh, not again? I'm still not sure that's a good idea,' complained Thomas. 'What if Hugh noticed you were there, somehow? If he can read minds, maybe he can see ... whatever you are, when your body isn't with you.'

'He can't, don't you worry. As it happens, he looked straight through me – it felt really odd. Anyway, Brian was interrogating Hugh for more information on how the green light works. He referred to it as the 'mind control continuum.' It is, and I quote; *a form of telepathic hypnosis via imperceptible pulses in light.*'

'Well!' exclaimed Thomas. 'I'm impressed! I'll have to read up on that next time I go to the library. Mind you, I can't say I've noticed a section devoted to telepathic hypnosis in the Bodleian.' Alice scowled at him.

Grandad carried on regardless. 'The medium, which in this case is the green light, is regularly charged by the warmth from hands. That's why the effect of the Egglos and Rowbots can last quite a while. Apparently the effects brought on by the fireworks and the large screen images are only short-term. But the message remains in the subconscious, so people continue to spread the word, or do as they are told. Just without the giggling or dazed expression.'

'So ... that means that the Egglos and Rowbots could actually be more harmful ... because their light is more powerful,' realised Thomas.

'Exactly,' agreed Alice, who obviously had no trouble understanding the explanation. 'Dad says the Egglos are already giving children headaches.'

'I'm not surprised,' replied Grandad.

'But what's it really for, this green light hypnosis?' demanded Alice impatiently.

'Brian and Hugh want to control people throughout their life. The reason they are targeting children is that the telepathic hypnosis has a greater effect, the younger the person. Hugh claims that the green light is addictive; these young people will want it in one form or another for the rest of their lives unless their exposure to it stops now.'

'Oh my life, that's awful!' whispered Alice.

'As children, the messages can influence them to pester their parents to buy things,' Grandad went on. 'When they get older, Hugh is planning to produce computer devices that do the same thing, influencing where they study, work and what they spend their money on – even what house they buy. Then he will be controlling the minds of adults as well as children.

Imagine a life where nothing is down to chance, nothing is coincidence. And there will be no such thing as free will.'

Grandma was standing in the doorway of the kitchen, wiping a tear from her eye with her apron. She couldn't bear the thought of children being manipulated.

'They really are twisted,' declared Thomas. 'Potentially, they could take over the world; we're dealing with real-life super-villains.'

'I'm afraid you're right,' replied Grandad. 'Their influence will quickly spread further afield. They've decided it will generate good publicity if they donate fireworks to large charity events – while transmitting whatever message they please to large gatherings. They're also planning to use them after concerts at the castle, when thousands of people are present. Most of those concerts are outdoor events in summer.'

Thomas slammed his mug down noisily. 'So what are we going to do about it? I just don't see how we can stop them without drawing attention to ourselves. We can't report technology that isn't exactly human, can we? We'd be putting Finwips at risk as well as the Sinwips. Not that I'm bothered about the latter.'

'I know,' said Grandad quietly. 'But there may be one solution. One that Imogen wouldn't approve of, so I don't think we should tell her about it.'

'What is it?' asked Alice, leaning forward.

'It's to do with you, Thomas,' he replied. 'Your ability, this telekinesis thing … I don't think it's as simple as that.'

'What do you mean?'

'Well … remember what you told me about the knight on its wooden horse in the Great Hall? How the horse was looking around, and the knight gripping the reins?'

'Of course,' he said with a smirk, as he recalled the incident.

'That wasn't just telekinesis.'

Thomas looked at him in trepidation, wondering what was coming next. Grandad scratched his beard – something he always did before he said something serious. 'Telekinesis can cause an object to move,' he began. 'Not *change*, just move. What you did at the castle that day was different. You made the horse and its rider come to life.'

A smile spread across Thomas's face. 'Yeah, right! And I suppose if I'd waited a moment longer, there would have been wooden droppings on the floor.'

Alice knew Grandad was right. It made perfect sense, and he didn't crack his face.

'I'm telling you the truth,' he said. 'If you had simply made it move, it would have slid along the floor in Hugh's direction with rigid legs, probably still fixed to its plinth. What you *actually* did was make it behave like a real horse. Its legs moved as though they had muscles; it's eyes focused on Hugh before it charged. And the knight held on for dear life because he knew what his horse was about to do! He wasn't just an empty suit of armour!'

Thomas's eyes looked as though they were going to pop out of his head onto his placemat. Alice had thrown her head back and was staring up at the ceiling. It was a shock, certainly, but it made her feel quite normal compared to her brother. Super-intelligence seemed far more normal than making inanimate objects come to life!

'Okaaay,' Thomas responded eventually. 'If that *is* the case, how does that help stop Hugh?'

'Right,' said Grandad, lowering his voice and looking over his shoulder to make sure Grandma wasn't listening. 'Remember your somewhat controversial suggestion of causing Hugh to have an accident, in the hope of hindering his concentration for a while?'

'I certainly do,' said Thomas.

'Well, I don't think it's so controversial now. I suspect that if he *were* injured more than you intended, you could put it right. If you can make a wooden horse and some pieces of metal function as they should, you can repair broken bones.'

'Wow!' shrieked Alice. Grandad frowned and put his finger to his lips – he certainly didn't want Grandma to hear this bit. 'Sorry,' she whispered. 'You mean like doing an operation without even touching him?'

'I think that's what he's getting at,' replied Thomas in disbelief. He was smitten with the idea, though. Firstly, he'd make sure Hugh got what he deserved. Then he could practise 'no hole' surgery. Perfect!

'Now, before you get carried away with this,' Grandad continued, 'it's only to be done as a last resort. If anyone can think of an alternative, preferably non-violent, we go with that instead. Plus, we need to wait for the right opportunity to do it. Otherwise it won't look like an accident.'

Thomas nodded thoughtfully.

'I'm worried about this opening day at the windmill on Friday,' said Alice. 'Do you think they'll try something with the green lights when all those businesspeople are there?'

'It's possible,' replied Grandad. 'Though I'm not sure they'd risk it – the press will be there, you see. They'll want as much coverage as possible in the newspapers. It wouldn't be ideal if Hugh's dodgy light show was photographed or filmed, would it?'

'I suppose not,' agreed Alice. 'And they can't use the fireworks because it's during the day.'

'Whatever happens,' said Grandad, 'we won't be there, we've no excuse to get in. And Hugh knows you're a Finwip now, so you can't go as Lucinda's friend.'

'Shame Mum didn't get an invitation through the funeral parlour,' said Thomas. 'She's a local businesswoman, but she didn't make it onto the guest list. Probably because Rowbottom's messages won't have much of an effect on her clients!'

They all laughed at that.

'Hey, you know who *could* be our eyes and ears at the open day!' Thomas suddenly remembered. 'Seb! He said he's going to be there with the cake. Obviously his mother can't attend because she'd be identified as one of us, and her colleague is on holiday.'

'It'll only take five minutes to carry a cake in from a van,' Alice pointed out.

'I know, but he has to stay with it. He said it's part of the service for a large cake. Apparently, he needs to attach the sails when it's in place, and then show Rowbottom how to cut it when the time comes.'

'Fantastic!' said Grandad, delighted by the news. Alice felt dreadful. Poor Seb, being stuck in that windmill with Brian and Hugh. Still, at least he'd have Lucinda to talk to. Brian always made sure his family was present at these events.

'I say we give Seb a few pointers on what to look out for, and make sure he sends us a message if he spots anything untoward,' said Grandad. 'We'll be waiting in the car nearby, at the ready just in case.'

'And what could we possibly do, if the green lights did appear?' asked Alice dismissively.

'Anything, as long as we interrupt proceedings,' replied Grandad. 'Run in and keel over, as if you're ill, shout something about a fire ... anything!'

Thomas smiled to himself. If things really kicked off at the windmill, he might have the opportunity to execute his plan. Alice wasn't convinced. She sighed loudly.

'Now, we say nothing of this to Imogen, agreed?' said Grandad. 'I'll tell her about the Rowbots and so on, but not about our little trip out on Friday. She might try and stop us. In fact, I know she will. I'll collect you at mid-day, it starts at one o'clock. And I'll tell your mum and dad I'm taking you out for lunch. That's true – I'll bring a packed lunch. We can eat it in the car.'

'Ooh, can't wait,' said Alice sarcastically. 'Oh no! Sarah will be with us! She's coming round on Friday.'

'That's alright, the more the merrier! She wouldn't want to be left out, would she?' laughed Grandad. 'Until then, as Imogen advised, stay vigilant. If you hear anything else at school, Alice, let me know. And keep an eye on your headmistress, Miss Poutwell; if she's got a special Rowbot, who knows what Hugh will make her do.'

'It's Miss Frownwell!' Alice corrected him.

'Whatever. Ah, here comes the cheesecake!' Grandma carried it to the table and sat down with them. Thomas insisted that they stayed to have a slice, then they would take some home with them. There was plenty for Seb and Sarah as well. When it was time to go, Alice's face still looked solemn. Grandma squeezed her hand.

'Promise me you'll be careful where this Hugh Rowbottom is concerned, Alice. I know I don't get involved in these matters much, but I understand more than I let on. Over the years I've learned a lot about Sinwips – with age comes wisdom. And this character really worries me.'

Alice nodded. 'OK,' she replied. 'I promise. Do you think I'll ever have a school holiday again that isn't spoiled by some Finwip/Sinwip hassle?' she asked wistfully.

'Of course, my love,' said Grandma, putting her arm round her. 'One day!'

'Oh, Alice, cheer up!' said Grandad. 'Look on the bright side!'

'What bright side?'

'Thomas tells me you've got a fantastic new wheelbarrow!'

She nearly threw the cheesecake at him, but it was too nice to waste.

*

'Listen, don't fret about this plan to wait outside the windmill,' said Thomas on the way home. 'We might not even have to go in. There's a chance that Hugh won't dare do anything to spoil the day.'

'Hmm. I know him better than you do,' Alice reminded him. 'It will be Good Friday. And I promise you, if he's involved, it definitely won't be good.'

Chapter 13

Cake and Cattle

Good Friday soon came round. Last day of term on Wednesday had been horrendous. The junior class with Rowbots had been made to spend the second half of their R.E. lesson standing in the playground after reading out every word backwards. Alice had heard that the children read in reverse with such ease that Mrs Knight had been terrified. Year 8 had a visit from Miss Frownwell about their dismal maths test results and their behaviour in science the day before. This time the Rowbots had told everyone to cut off a lock of their hair and hold it in the Bunsen flame with tongs. Mrs Dawkins' textbook said to use a piece of bread – they were supposed to be measuring energy in food. Instead of smelling like burnt toast, the science lab stank of sulphurous burning hair. Miss Frownwell obviously didn't see the connection between the Rowbots and general mayhem. She ended the 'ticking off' by telling the class that the whole school would have Rowbots by September if she had her way; they were invaluable.

'No prize for guessing the message that her Rowbot's transmitting,' said Alice.

Just after mid-day a burgundy Morris Minor was parked in a layby near Clifton Windmill. Grandad, Thomas, Alice and Sarah were munching thoughtfully on sandwiches, wondering what was happening in the Windmill Restaurant. They had seen a few deliveries arriving, along with photographers and local radio vehicles. Anna had already dropped Seb off with the windmill cake. She waved at them as she drove past – Seb had informed her of their plan, which made her feel much better about leaving him there.

Lucinda had come out to meet Seb, and was very excited to see the cake. It really was a perfect replica of the windmill.

Anna was reluctant to get out of the van in case she was spotted by Brian or Hugh, but fortunately Lucinda wanted to help Seb carry the cake indoors. When he returned to the van to pick up the sails, he promised his mother he would be careful, and patted his mobile phone in his pocket. Alice and Thomas were on speed-dial.

Inside the building, after twenty minutes of fiddling with the sails, Seb managed to attach them successfully to the cake. Wearing a blue shirt and cravat, with matching 'Magical Creations' apron, he leaned back against the wall by the cake. He looked around the brand new dining room, which was elegantly decorated for the occasion, with plenty of fresh flowers and about a hundred bottles of champagne ready in ice buckets on the tables. Lucinda reappeared from the kitchens.

'Come and see the food!' she called to Seb, beckoning him over excitedly. 'It looks brilliant!'

Seb followed her, looking over his shoulder at the windmill cake to make sure it was safe. The catering certainly looked good – tray after tray of savoury and sweet delicacies were laid out in the kitchen.

'Just how many guests are you expecting?' he asked Lucinda.

'Hundreds I think, judging by all this food.' As they admired it, the chefs started to walk out of the back door.

'Where are they all going?' asked Seb.

'Er, I don't … oooh! The balloon delivery is here! They must be helping to bring them in. I can't wait to see them!' She hurried after them.

Seb remained in the kitchen. He noticed the storeroom door was open, and couldn't resist having a nose at all their cooking ingredients. What a stash of chocolate! A crash coming from the main kitchen area made him jump. He peered around the storeroom door. Someone had dropped a ladle. It was Hugh Rowbottom! Alice had described him in detail, from the cropped blonde hair and green eyes, to his pale face with the scar on his chin. That was definitely him, dressed in black as usual.

Hugh looked all around to make sure he was alone, then took a small bottle from his pocket. It was a round-bottomed flask containing a bright green liquid. Using a pipette, Hugh proceeded to add one drop of the liquid to each portion of food. Moving swiftly, he was doing whole trays within seconds, glancing over his shoulder to make sure no one could see him.

He was contaminating the food. The green liquid looked suspiciously similar to the green light. This was something new – what if it was dangerous?

Silently, Seb began to type a text message to Alice, his fingers trembling as he pressed the keys. 'Hugh spiking foo …' Then he heard Hugh walking out of the doors into the dining room. The cake! Seb hurtled out of the storeroom, through the kitchen doors and overtook Hugh as he raced to reach his cake. Hugh stopped dead and stared at him.

'Just needed some water,' spluttered Seb, red-faced. 'It's against company policy to leave the cakes unattended before cutting.'

Hugh smirked. 'Really?' he replied, slipping the bottle into the inner pocket of his jacket.

'Can't be too careful,' said Seb.

Hugh sat down at the table nearest to the cake. 'That's pretty good,' he said smoothly. 'I'm sure the children will love it.'

'Oh! I … I had no idea that children were coming,' mumbled Seb. What if they had a reaction to whatever Hugh had put in the food?

'Why don't you go and get some of those balloons and tie them to your cake table?' suggested Hugh with a smile. 'That would set it off nicely.'

'You do have some interesting ideas, sir,' replied Seb. 'But I really shouldn't leave the cake. You could get some for me, though.' He could be as slimy as Hugh, if he wanted to – what he really needed was the chance to finish that text.

Hugh merely grunted and looked out of the window. The guests were starting to arrive. A lady got out of the first car carrying a toddler. Her husband joined her with a little girl who looked about four years old. Seb felt a vibration in his pocket. He took out his phone and saw a message from Alice.

'On our way!'

Thank goodness! He must have pressed send before he finished it.

Hugh spun round. 'Is something wrong?' he asked.

'Not at all!' replied Seb. 'I see you have guests arriving, sir.'

If looks could kill, Seb would have been on the floor. Hugh's green eyes had shot daggers at him. He stormed over to the door, changing his distorted, angry face into a fake smile just in time to greet the young family. 'Welcome to the Windmill Restaurant!' he beamed. 'How lovely to see you all!'

Brian Rowbottom came marching through the dining room from his office to join him, his enormous black moustache glistening as if he'd waxed it for the occasion. Photographers and journalists followed him out of the office and began to assemble their equipment around a small stage that had been set up with a microphone. Seb shuddered. It wasn't a nice feeling, knowing that you were in the company of people who had kidnapped your grandfather not so long ago …

*

The Morris arrived in the car park, skidding on the gravel as Grandad parked it in haste. He had decided to let Imogen know that hundreds of people were at risk thanks to Hugh's latest creation. He couldn't keep something as important as that to himself. For a few seconds, he and his passengers looked out of the windows. Cars were now pouring in through the gates, and many more guests had brought their children with them. Grandad was mortified.

'We need to stop these people from getting in,' he said. 'They might start on the food straight away. I think I'll head round the back and see if I can get in without being seen. Thomas, you'll need to hold the kitchen doors shut to prevent them carrying the food out.'

One minute Alice was gazing at the stream of vehicles, the next, in the opposite direction, across the fields. 'I've got an idea!' she said suddenly, jumping out of the car. 'Sarah, get ready to guard the gates to stop them getting out!' she shouted as she ran off.

'Stop who getting out?' asked Sarah, baffled, but doing as she was told anyway. She watched as Alice climbed over a low fence and hared across the nearest field. In the distance she saw her pause by a herd of cows. 'What on earth is she doing?' she muttered to herself.

Alice had decided she would finally put her 'animal communication' to the test. It was a long shot, but if these cows could understand her as well as Jack could, or Faunus, she might be able to persuade them to wreak havoc in the car park, and prevent people from entering the windmill. She did feel an idiot shouting at ninety-odd Friesians in the middle of a field, and sincerely hoped the farmer wasn't around. The response was some disgruntled mooing, then most of them carried on eating grass. It wasn't working. Perhaps it had just been coincidence with the other animals. Now Alice felt really stupid. One cow wandered off away from the rest, followed by one or two more. Their pace quickened, then more cows began to join them. They were heading towards the windmill!

'Are you helping me? Did you understand?' yelled Alice like a loony.

'MOO!' replied the cow leading the attack.

Alice punched the air in triumph. 'Yes!' she shouted to herself, running after the thundering herd of cows. She could only imagine how ridiculous she looked at that moment. As they neared the fence around the car park, the first cow lowered her head and charged at it. The wooden rails smashed easily, allowing the rest of the cows to pile in behind her.

Sarah stood at the gate, rooted to the spot. She hated to admit it, but at that moment she was terrified of cows. And who wouldn't be if a whole herd was galloping towards them? What was Alice playing at? What on earth was she thinking?

'Don't let them get out onto the road!' shouted Alice. Sarah threw her hands in the air. How could she stop a huge cow from doing as it pleased? They didn't understand *her*.

The herd split up, wandering between the parked cars and causing the cars driving in to brake suddenly. There was a loud crunch as an expensive-looking sports car ploughed into the back of a Jaguar. The drivers didn't get out, though; no one dared to emerge from their vehicle for fear of being trampled by cows. Alice was loving every minute. One cow was scratching its backside on a gleaming silver Range Rover. Two others were chomping on the miniature trees in pots outside the front door of the restaurant.

Meanwhile, Thomas had been peering through a window and spotted the doors to the kitchen. He concentrated on them for a moment, then they slammed shut. There was shouting from the kitchen as a couple of waiters attempted to kick them open, but they wouldn't budge. Thomas had made sure they were held fast. One waiter carried two trays out of the back door and began to walk round to the front. He changed his mind when he was met by a cow. Grandad had slipped in through the same door, but when he realised just how many staff there were, and how noisy it was in the kitchen, he knew he couldn't make himself heard if he tried to explain. He looked at all the food laid out. Then he spied a fire extinguisher. He yanked it from its stand and ran across the kitchen, dowsing the trays of food with white foam.

'Fire!' he shouted. 'Fire! Everybody out!'

'STOP!' yelled Jeremy Rowbottom. 'My food! What are you doing?'

'What I have to do,' shouted Grandad. 'I'm sorry.'

A stampede began as the other chefs and waiting staff abandoned what they were doing and dashed to the back door. There was a scream as someone was nearly knocked off her feet. It was Mrs Rowbottom.

Covered with foam himself, Grandad offered his arm to steady her. She stared at him in horror.

'You must be Jacqueline Rowbottom,' he said. 'You don't know me, but I have good reason to believe that your nephew has contaminated this food. And there are children present.' As soon as he'd said it, he bit his lip. Why should she believe him? He was a complete stranger, and here he was accusing Hugh of something dreadful.

Mrs Rowbottom's mouth fell open. Hugh suddenly appeared behind her.

'I'll kill you, you old busybody!' he snarled, pointing his finger at Grandad.

'Not if I kill you first!' shouted his uncle Jeremy, seizing a carving knife. 'You'll pay for this!'

Mrs Rowbottom squealed with rage and grabbed a stainless steel cleaver from the wall. She swung it at Hugh, but he ducked. 'How could you?' she screamed.

'Easily!' laughed Hugh, dashing outside. 'It only takes a few drops!' Tearing round the side of the windmill, he ground to a halt. His precious Aston Martin was surrounded by cattle. One cow had its front hooves on the bonnet. Another was in the middle of producing a steaming pile behind the car, which splattered nicely up the paintwork. That particular animal appeared to be smiling at him. 'AAARGH!' he shouted, throwing his scrawny arms in the air and running back in the direction he had come from.

Alice caught sight of him running away and followed. Several chefs as well as Mrs Rowbottom were in hot pursuit, armed with kitchen knives. He began to climb the metal ladder up the side of the windmill. 'If anyone tries to follow me, I'll push them off!' he yelled.

Thomas appeared when he heard all the shouting.

'Where have you been?' snapped Grandad. 'Have you locked the front doors as well, to keep the journalists inside?'

He nodded, and looked up. Hugh was nearly as high as the roof. 'He might jump!' said Thomas.

'Well, that'll solve that, then,' replied Grandad.

'Maybe, but we don't want blood on our hands,' Thomas pointed out. 'We'd have to answer some very awkward questions. I'd better go up after him.'

'NO!' roared Grandad. 'Leave him be, for now. Everyone back inside, please. I know we're all angry, but let's give the boy space to calm down.'

'If this is true, that headcase could have cost us our jobs!' ranted a young trainee chef, wringing his hands in distress. 'We've spent days creating those dishes, and they could have made people ill!'

'Believe me, I'll make *him* ill when I get hold of him,' growled Jeremy.

'I'll call the police,' said Mrs Rowbottom. 'Hugh should be arrested. I've never trusted him, but Brian just wouldn't listen. He won't hear a bad word about that boy.'

'Please, don't,' begged Grandad. 'Er … it won't look good if the police are called to the opening day of your restaurant, will it?'

Mrs Rowbottom sighed and put her phone away. Grudgingly, and still gripping their weapons, the group made its way back into the kitchen. At the nod from his grandad, Thomas slammed the door shut behind them. They sighed in relief, though Mrs Rowbottom could still be heard squawking and banging on the door.

'Where's Alice?' asked Thomas.

During the kerfuffle, Alice had seized her opportunity and was now nearly at the top of the ladder.

'Please, no!' gasped Grandad. Thomas grabbed the bottom rung to follow her.

'Don't you dare!' insisted his grandad. 'Your wings won't help you if you fall.'

*

Alice finally reached the top and peered over the roof. Hugh was standing on the far side of it, looking down at the chaos in the car park. She climbed up on to the small circular roof, which appeared to be coated in metal; the sound of her feet alerted Hugh to her arrival. He charged across the roof towards her, full of rage.

'You've ruined everything!' he snarled, before dropping to his knees. Alice noticed movement in his jacket, then his wings tore through it. They were nasty, thin wings, like those of a daddy-long-legs. She recoiled at the sight of them. Hugh recovered in seconds, leaping up to push Alice to the floor. Flat on her back, she growled in temper and thumped the roof with her fists. As she clambered to her feet, her own wings erupted, ripping through her jacket.

'Oh no, not another one,' she muttered. She'd soon run out of clothes at this rate. Hugh was in a crouching position, staring at her from a few feet away. The spindly wings, along with his bony frame dressed in black, created an evil-looking human insect. He couldn't help but stare enviously at Alice's enormous wings. She felt braver now that they had appeared – at least she could save herself if she slipped. It looked as though Hugh was preparing to lunge at her. Something glinted in the sun; he had his silver penknife in his hand. Darting into the air in terror, Alice hovered just above him – the flying practice had paid off. It certainly felt good looking down at him. 'You took things too far!' she shouted. 'Brainwashing people into spending money is one thing, but trying to control children?'

Hugh tried to swipe at her, stamping his feet in frustration. 'I'm going to rule the world! You can't stop me!' he yelled.

Alice couldn't help smiling as she thought of Thomas's 'super-villain' comments. She noticed a creaking sound, and realised that the sails of the windmill were slowly starting to move. Hugh had his back to them. 'You interfered with food when you had no idea of the effects,' she ranted. 'I bet you haven't tested it. Small children were going to eat it! You're sick!'

'Oh, I have tested it. Only once, though. Your chums at school certainly seemed to like it in chocolate. You could say their little faces 'lit up!'' He cackled uncontrollably, in hysterics at his own joke. 'They had a double dose of my medicine – lights as well as food!'

No wonder they were being so strange that day. 'What did you put in the food?' demanded Alice.

'It doesn't matter,' he replied. 'Everyone needs to learn.'

'It does matter. Tell me what it is!' she shrieked, flapping her immense wings and circling around his head like an enormous vulture.

This was torture for Hugh. He was flailing his arms around in temper, livid at being interrogated by a thirteen-year-old girl. 'It's this!' he yelled, putting down his knife and retrieving the bottle from the remains of his jacket. 'It's a responsive liquid, the first of its kind,' he announced proudly in his haunting voice. 'One drop of this, and the consumer will do the bidding of the person who applied it. Would you like some, Alice?' he asked with a twisted smile.

Alice swooped down and tried to kick the bottle from his hands. She missed, much to his amusement, but as Hugh dodged her foot, he accidentally knocked his penknife off the roof. He growled. 'You must learn as well,' he warned.

'Learn what?'

'That we are superior beings. We have evolved to dominate. For some reason, you Finwips choose to do nothing with your abilities. I pity you.'

Alice scowled. 'You've evolved to be evil, that's all. To think I defended you at first! I thought you were a magician!'

'And how right you were, my dear, clever little Alice. But not just any magician. I am a MIND MAGICIAN!' he shouted. With that, he picked up a length of metal pipe lying on the roof and jumped up at her, waving it above his head insanely. 'Nothing and no one stands in my way!'

Chapter 14

Thomas Works his Magic

'What you are, is a psycho!' declared Thomas, his face appearing at the top of the ladder. 'Alice, are you alright?'

As she turned to look at him, Hugh managed to grab her foot and dragged her down roughly. She landed on the roof with a thud and he pinned her to the floor, wielding the metal pipe ready to strike her.

'Get away from her!' roared Thomas, clambering onto the roof. 'What sort of man fights a young girl?' he demanded. 'You disgust me.'

As Hugh stood up to face him, seething with rage, Thomas took his chance. 'Stay down, Alice,' he instructed, as a deafening creak followed by a crash drowned out his words. One of the windmill's sails had broken off and came hurtling down towards them. There was a sickening thud as it clipped Hugh on the back of the head and he fell to the ground. His wings retracted instantly. Alice screamed. Another scream in the distance told her that Sarah had seen it from the car park.

'What were you playing at, Alice? Fancy following that nutter – you could have been killed!' ranted Thomas.

'Are you alright?' came a shout. Imogen and Anna were flying towards them riding Guinevere and Kallisto. Grandad had hitched a ride with Imogen, out of his mind with worry since his grandchildren had been up there with the 'psycho'. Alice smiled at the sight of the two unicorns, their wings gleaming in the spring sunshine.

'I think so,' replied Alice, groaning and grasping her left wrist as she sat up. 'Oh blimey, did anyone see you?' she asked. 'I can't believe they're out in broad daylight!'

'Well, Anna offered to drive her van, but when your grandad said there was another tall building involved, I wasn't taking any chances!' Imogen replied. 'I didn't even stop to remove their headdresses. It's OK, we didn't fly past the car park. No one has seen us, we've flown over fields all the way.'

Guinevere and Kallisto landed carefully on the roof, their hooves clattering on the metal. Grandad jumped down and hurried over to Alice, while Imogen ran to Hugh's motionless body.

'Oh, no! At least he's alive,' said Imogen, checking his pulse. 'What are we going to do? We can't call an ambulance for him.'

'Just wait a moment,' said Grandad. 'Thomas, I think Alice has broken her wrist.'

Alice was bright red, fighting back the tears as she tried to put on a brave face. Her wrist was agony. She must have landed on it when Hugh pulled her down.

'Do your best, Thomas,' pleaded Grandad.

Hesitantly, Alice held out her wrist. Thomas knelt down, supported it in his hands, and concentrated on it intently.

'What's going on?' demanded Imogen.

'Shhh,' whispered Anna.

All eyes were on Alice's wrist. As they watched, it became very red, and she felt a burning sensation. Suddenly she yelped in pain and withdrew her wrist from Thomas's hands.

'Oh no, I'm so sorry!' he blurted out. 'I didn't mean to hurt you.'

Alice rubbed the hot skin on her wrist, a tear running down her cheek. Then she moved her hand around gently. It didn't hurt. She waved her hand around in a circular motion.

'It's better!' she shrieked. 'You've fixed it!' She gave Thomas a hug. He was flushed with embarrassment, but at the same time looked elated that he had cured Alice's injury. Grandad couldn't stop smiling.

'Er, what just happened here?' asked Imogen, hardly daring to believe her eyes. 'Did you really just heal a broken wrist by concentrating on it, Thomas?'

He nodded. 'It certainly looks that way. I thought I could just move objects, but Grandad noticed I could actually bring things to life. Well, make them function as they should, anyway.'

Imogen shook her head in disbelief. 'That's incredible. I … I don't know what to say.'

'I do,' said Grandad. 'Get over to Hugh, Thomas, and fix his head!'

'Wait!' said Alice, getting to her feet. She leaned over Hugh and found the small bottle. 'Thank goodness it didn't break!' she muttered. 'Hugh said this is a 'responsive liquid'. Whatever that is. Apparently, the person who adds the drops decides on the effect it will have.'

'I'm not sure I approve of this,' said Imogen. But she did nothing to intervene.

Thomas studied the liquid. 'Do you think it will work on a Sinwip?' he asked.

'I'll give him plenty to make sure!' replied Alice, already removing the pipette from the bottle and crouching down to open Hugh's mouth. She muttered a few words which Thomas couldn't quite make out, before letting six drops fall onto Hugh's tongue. When she stepped back, Thomas examined his head. Some blood could be seen trickling through his blonde hair. He stared at it for a moment, then closed his eyes. Everyone was silent. After a while, he opened his eyes and held his hands just above Hugh's head.

'That's it,' Thomas announced. 'I've done all I can, but I've no idea if it will work. I've never had to heal someone's head before.'

'That's not a nice one to begin with, either,' said Grandad.

Hugh suddenly gave a moan. Imogen squeezed his hand. 'Are you alright?' she whispered.

He blinked, dazzled by the sunlight, and looked thoroughly confused to see everyone. 'Where are we?' he asked, staring in bewilderment at Guinevere and Kallisto.

'We're on the roof of the windmill,' replied Alice bluntly. 'Don't you remember?'

Hugh seemed surprised and looked all around. 'Um ... yes ... I think I do.' He hid his face in his hands. 'I'm so sorry,' he said quietly. 'To everyone.'

Grandad winked at Thomas. Imogen smiled.

'Whatever did you order that liquid to do?' whispered Anna.

'From now on, Hugh should always act in the best interests of other people,' said Alice. 'I don't think he'll give us any trouble for a while.'

'Just as well. Good for you,' said Anna.

Guinevere and Kallisto carried them all back down to the ground. Alice would have preferred to fly down, but daren't, in case someone saw her from a window. Before Thomas left the roof, she saw him remove something from the tip of the fallen sail and conceal it under his sweatshirt.

Imogen passed round her blue spray, so that Alice and the unicorns could retract their wings. Then Grandad gave Thomas the final nod. 'Better let them all out,' he grinned. 'Poor Seb's been stuck in there with them for ages! Then get ready to run – we can't let Brian see us.'

People surged out as soon as the doors flew open. Grandad wrestled with Mrs Rowbottom to extract the cleaver from her grip. Then he, Thomas and Anna ran as fast as they could towards the Morris. Hugh was sitting on the grass in a daze.

Lucinda and Seb ran out behind the kitchen staff. 'WOW!' gasped Lucinda, suddenly noticing Guinevere and Kallisto. 'There are two of them! I can't believe it, they're so beautiful! Even better than the photo!' She ran over and stroked Guinevere's nose.

Imogen and Alice smiled. 'Well, it had to happen one day!' said Alice.

Finally, Brian emerged, his face the colour of a beetroot. Alice tried to hide behind Kallisto.

'What on EARTH has been going on?' he shouted. 'First we were invaded by a herd of cows, then all the doors seized up and we were trapped inside with a handful of terrified guests! I've never been so embarrassed! I had to pacify them with champagne and cake!' He looked down his nose at Hugh. 'And what happened to you?'

'If you don't mind, I'm going to take the rest of the day off,' said Hugh weakly. 'I don't feel too good.' He stood up and walked away in the direction of his car. Alice followed, leading Kallisto by the reins. The cows were gradually making their way back into the field. Sarah was running around looking exhausted.

'Oh, about time!' she ranted when she caught sight of Alice. 'Do I look like a sheep-dog? Or whatever rounds up cows?' She stopped when she noticed Kallisto, who was eyeing up the cattle suspiciously. 'Oh!'

A tall man in a suit came running out of the front door. 'Hugh! What's been happening?' he called, running towards him.

'I'd rather not talk about it now, Dad,' he replied. He got into his car and spotted Brian hurrying after him, waving his fists. Mrs Rowbottom must have explained what had happened – she appeared behind him with Jeremy.

'Sort your son out, Pat!' bellowed Jeremy. 'Otherwise I will.'

Hugh revved the engine and put it into reverse. Before he shot off, the back wheels spun in the enormous cow pat that had been deposited earlier, leaving his poor father showered in … the brown stuff.

Brian turned the corner and stared in horror at the dripping, stinking figure before him. He held his nose. 'Pat?' he said in bewilderment.

His unfortunate brother wiped his face and opened his eyes. 'I'm afraid that's exactly what it was, Brian.'

*

'I'm sorry things didn't go well today, Lucinda,' said Alice sympathetically. 'It's a shame Hugh turned out to be … well, a problem.'

Lucinda wrinkled up her nose. 'Oh, that's no surprise. Mum and I have never liked him anyway,' she admitted, as she wandered off to join her father.

Alice smiled. Seb appeared next to her, and they waved to Imogen before she galloped off into the distance.

'Unbelievable!' exclaimed Seb. 'All this excitement, and I was left out again. You've all been out here, where the action was happening, and I've been stuck in there in this stupid outfit serving cake to grumpy toffs!'

'You're lucky!' Sarah remarked, checking the soles of her shoes. 'I've been chasing stinking great cows! One man shouted at me when one of them knocked his wing mirror off! As if it was my fault!'

By now the guests were leaving in droves – they couldn't get away fast enough. 'I'd better go, too,' said Seb. 'Are you riding back, Sarah?'

She nodded and climbed onto Kallisto behind Alice. They all headed over to the Morris.

'Where's Thomas gone?' asked Grandad, as Seb opened the door to get in.

'I thought he was with you!' replied Alice.

'He was for a second, then he jumped out again and said he'd forgotten something. What's he up to now?'

Alice was horrified. Just as they were ready to go, and she thought it was over, Thomas had gone back in. She could only guess he'd gone to the room at the top of the windmill to look around in Hugh's workshop.

'I think I know,' she said. 'I'll be back in a minute.' With that, she jumped down from Kallisto and ran back into the restaurant, making sure the Rowbottoms didn't see her. They were having a heated argument with a guest whose car had been damaged by the cows.

At the far end of the dining room, Alice hurried up the spiral staircase until she reached the fourth floor, feeling rather dizzy. There she found Thomas in what appeared to be a science laboratory. This round room had exposed brick walls, partly covered in curved bookshelves. They were laden with books, paperwork and rocks of various shapes and colours, along with jars of dried leaves and what appeared to be seeds.

'What's all this?' she asked, looking around in amazement.

'It looks like Hugh practises a bit of biochemistry as well!' replied Thomas. 'I've never seen so much equipment apart from at uni; this must be what was inside all the crates that started to arrive in December. I do believe Hugh fancies himself as an alchemist! He made the green liquid himself. This is distillation apparatus.' It was still warm to the touch. Next to it was a bottle of 'Distilled Dartmoor Spring Water,' and lying on the bench, some green stuff and a scalpel. 'Gingko leaves!' said Thomas, picking one up. There were some spiky pieces too, in a jar labelled 'Araucaria araucana.' 'The needles from a monkey puzzle tree!' said Thomas. 'What a combination!'

'Oh dear,' whispered Alice.

'What?'

'I forgot to tell you I saw Hugh collecting leaves from the trees in Brian's garden. I didn't think it was important.'

'So that's where they came from. Two of the oldest and toughest trees in the world. No wonder that liquid was so powerful. It doesn't matter, Alice. I'd never have guessed what he was doing with them.' He studied the equipment carefully, then paused at a large glass flask. There was something bulky lying in the bottom of it, where the distilled green liquid could pass over it before the process was complete. Thomas removed the flask and extracted the object with a pair of tongs. When he held it up, Alice wasn't sure whether he was going to laugh or cry.

'What is it?' she asked, frowning at the dull brown object he'd retrieved.

'It's another piece of this,' he replied, taking a larger chunk out of his pocket. 'I found this fixed to the sail that fell down. There's one attached to each.' He handed it to Alice.

'It's not ... oh, please tell me it's not another one of the stones Grandad was talking about!' she pleaded.

'It's one and the same,' replied Thomas gravely. 'It seems Hugh is an expert in harnessing the forces of nature. Just like the folk of Arcanum Cove. Perhaps he thought that by raising the stones high in the sky, and exposing them to the elements up there, they'd become more powerful. He's tried everything: sun, rain, wind, kinetic energy from the sails ...'

'He might be right, for all we know,' said Alice quietly. 'That liquid certainly does something, and it was passed over a piece of the stone.'

'But where did he learn all this?' asked Thomas, saying aloud what they were both wondering as they looked all around. A small notebook on the floor caught Alice's eye – it must have fallen off the bench where Hugh had been working. 'Secrets of the Stones,' she read scrawled on the cover. It looked old; all the entries were hand-written in badly faded ink. She flicked through from cover to cover.

'It's all in here,' she said, stunned by what she had gleaned in those few seconds. 'History, stories, experiments and instructions. We've got a lot to learn.' She hid the notebook inside her jacket.

'You just read that entire book, didn't you! You never said you could speed-read!'

'Sometimes I wouldn't call it speed-reading. I don't even need to see all the pages. I just ... absorb it, somehow.'

Thomas smiled. 'You certainly are a strange one!' He stuffed the gingko leaves into his pocket and grabbed the jar of monkey puzzle needles. 'Come on, we'd better go before someone sees us. I'll come back for the other three stones on the sails later.'

They crept cautiously back down the stairs. No one was in the restaurant, so they walked out calmly.

'Thank goodness!' exclaimed Grandad. 'Now get in the car, Thomas, where I can keep an eye on you! Alice, you follow on that horse ... I mean unicorn, with Sarah. We'll see you at the village – no detours!'

Alice nodded as Grandad drove off with Thomas, Anna and Seb safely inside. Kallisto turned and trotted past Lucinda so that Alice could wave goodbye. Lucinda was now standing with her devastated father and Uncle Pat. She waved and smiled, even though she was next to that dreadful stench.

'I'm so glad Alice brought her horse!' grinned Lucinda. 'I've been looking forward to seeing it for ages! Dad? Are you alright?' She tapped him on the arm.

Brian appeared to be staring in to space. 'Er ... yes ...,' he mumbled. 'Seems like a nice girl.'

Alice couldn't believe what she had just overheard. Brian obviously had no idea that she rescued Theo. Hugh couldn't have told him. Which meant Brian hadn't sent him to Finwip village! They could all breathe a sigh of relief – the village was safe for now. Alice set off across the fields. Thankfully, she didn't have to worry about the direction – Kallisto knew the way.

Chapter 15

Plans for the Summer

Alice banged on Thomas's bedroom door at ten o'clock on Easter Sunday morning. 'Wake up! We're going somewhere, remember? And we need to be back for dinner! Grandma and Grandad are coming.'

No reply.

'If you don't come out now, I'm going to eat your Easter egg. I've finished mine already.'

There was a thud as Thomas jumped out of bed and opened the door. 'You dare!' he warned.

'Ooh, you look rough!' said Alice. 'How did you and Grandad get on last night?'

'Come in and I'll tell you,' yawned Thomas.

'Phew! It smells like something died in here.'

'Feel free to leave.'

Alice didn't move.

'Well,' began Thomas, 'I crept out when everyone was in bed, and Grandad collected me down the road. Then we waited in the usual layby. From there, we could see that the lights were still on at the windmill. Brian finally locked up and left just after midnight.' He paused for another yawn and a stretch. 'Anyway, I went round the back with a powerful flashlight. I had hoped to aim the beam on each sail in turn, so that I could concentrate on the stones and make them fall to the ground. Only, it didn't really work.'

'Why not?' asked Alice.

'The light wasn't strong enough to illuminate the sails from the ground, so I had to climb up the ladder again – which wasn't ideal in the dark with that cumbersome torch. Even then, I found it difficult to focus my mind by torchlight. Eventually, I managed it, and the first stone broke free from its binding and hit the ground. Luckily, Grandad was standing well out of the way! The second and third were easy after that. I put them in my rucksack and we drove home with our haul.'

'Oh no, they're not here, are they?' asked Alice anxiously. 'I don't want to be anywhere near them!'

'No. Grandad has hidden them in his garden. The one from his living room had already been relegated to the shed. Anyway, they can't hurt you, silly.'

'Maybe not. But I want to know more about them before I see them again.' She moved towards the door. 'Hurry up, then.'

'I'll be down in a minute. Get Jack ready, we'll have to take him with us, there's no other excuse to go out this morning.'

Alice liked the sound of that. She was sure Jack would love the village, but couldn't imagine how they would get him in the tree lift. By the time she had found his lead and prepared a bag of her home-grown produce, Thomas was ready, and he told their parents they were taking Jack for a long walk.

Alice had heard all about 'Easter Sunday Breakfast' in the village and was looking forward to it. Shame she'd have to restrain herself, she had to save room for a roast dinner this afternoon. At the oak tree, Thomas advised her to get into the lift first and put her back to the wall. Then she had to persuade Jack to get in and stand up, putting his paws above her shoulders. Not an easy manoeuvre, but he wouldn't fit in otherwise. Of course, he did as she asked. Now that they could understand each other, he trusted her completely.

Alice and Jack travelled down while Thomas waited on the pavement. Freya was just walking past in the corridor when the door of the lift opened. She couldn't believe her eyes when she saw a dog the size of a small pony towering over Alice in that cramped lift. Jack turned his head and grinned at her. Alice helped him reverse out of the door before he could jump down.

'Good morning, sir!' said Freya, stroking Jack's head. 'Are you our latest member? Welcome to the village, I think you're going to be very popular!'

Alice waited for Thomas before getting changed – it seemed only right that Jack joined him in the male changing rooms. When she put on her Finwip robes and let her wings out, she was amazed to see that the damage caused by the broken glass had healed completely. In just a week!

She joined Thomas and Jack in the dining room. It looked as good as it had at Christmas! It was difficult to say who was more surprised by what they saw; Alice or Jack. They looked around at a room full of Finwips with their wings on display and tables laden with food. Dotted around were large pots containing tree branches decorated with flowers and coloured eggs. Fay was wandering around with a tray of muffins. She hadn't been down to the village for a while, and couldn't understand why no one wanted one of her cakes. They were beautifully decorated, but unfortunately the icing was lime green and topped with shiny green eggs. Alice thought it was hilarious and ate one anyway, but Fay wasn't amused when they explained what had happened with Hugh. She looked at her cakes in dismay.

'I can't believe I've been stuck at work and missed it all!' she moaned. 'Apart from when you smashed the window at the cafe, of course.'

'What?' said Imogen, pricking her ears up as she came over to meet Jack.

'It was an accident,' said Alice quickly, not wanting to spoil Imogen's impression of her 'brave' encounter with Hugh.

Anna, Seb and Theo appeared armed with boxes from 'Magical Creations.' Grandma and Grandad Parker arrived at the same time, and couldn't wait to look inside the boxes. The first one Anna opened contained an enormous simnel cake. Grandad was impressed.

'Mine's a large slice of that one!' he announced.

'What else have you got for us, Seb?' asked Alice, rubbing her hands.

Seb fetched another box and grinned as he opened it. 'No, Alice, it's not another sweet pizza. Chocolate birds' nests with eggs and chicks!'

'These are great!' said Alice, helping herself to one. She felt embarrassed that she'd only brought vegetables. Spring greens and sprouting broccoli couldn't compete with cakes. But Rose, the school dinner lady, seemed very pleased with them.

'No Sarah today?' asked Grandad, settling down with a piece of cake.

'No,' replied Alice, putting a bowl of water down for Jack. 'She's gone out for the day with her family. She was really disappointed she couldn't make it.'

'Never mind, we'll take her a goody bag,' said Grandad. 'Make sure you eat your dinner, after all this,' he added, watching her eat another green muffin.

'Funny, Dad said you used to tell him that. I can't believe you weren't more careful what you told him, as a child. He said you could smell sweets on his breath when he turned into your road! Surely he guessed you weren't normal?'

Grandad laughed. 'I could never smell his sweets!' he chuckled. 'But I could see the top of the paper bag sticking out of his pocket!'

'What a mean trick!' groaned Alice, feeling a bit silly. Perhaps it was just her with the extreme sense of smell.

'You're right about your grandad not being normal, though!' Grandma assured her.

Freya joined them and handed Alice a small parcel. 'From Sarah,' she said. 'She asked me to give it to you today.'

Surprised, Alice tore open the paper. She pulled out a swimming costume. It had a strategically-positioned cross-shaped panel on the back to hide her wing base mark. 'Just what I need!' she said. 'Sarah kept her word! Thanks, Freya.'

'Now all you need is another invitation to Lucinda's house!' laughed Thomas.

'Er, I think I'll give it a miss for a while.'

Imogen stood up to say a few words; she wished everyone a happy Easter and assured them that the village was safe again. 'Recent events have been resolved,' she confirmed. 'Thanks to the Parker family, again, and Sebastian Seaton, of course!' Anna and Theo were very proud that Seb had done his bit for the village. He looked very pleased with himself when everyone clapped. Alice knew it bothered him that he wasn't a Finwip. Afterwards, he gave her a small box.

'I pinched a slice of windmill cake for you,' he said. 'I guessed you'd want to try it!'

'Thanks, Seb!' she grinned. But when she opened the box, she looked worried. 'Oh no, Seb, I thought you guarded the cake!' she whispered.

'I did! Oh … well … I only left it for a couple of minutes while I went into the kitchen with Lucinda.'

'Hugh got to the cake,' said Alice. 'I can smell the green liquid in it. How many people ate it?'

'Not that many,' replied Seb, panic-stricken. 'There were only two families in there when Thomas locked us in. And the journalists. And the Rowbottoms. And … me. Oh, Alice, don't tell my mum, she'll go mad!'

'OK, OK, I won't,' she whispered. 'I don't suppose you want to buy one of Brian's houses, do you?'

'What are you talking about?' asked Seb, thoroughly confused.

'Oh, never mind. Grandad suspected that the green drops were programmed to make anyone who ate them want to buy one of Rowbottom's properties. But it can't be that.'

'Well, I hope those young children who had a slice aren't trying to buy one!' replied Seb. 'Oh no, I wonder what's happened to *them*?'

'Look, don't panic. I'm sure we'll find out somehow,' said Alice. 'Go and have something to eat.' Seb nodded and wandered off. Alice went back to her family's table and sat down.

'So,' began Grandma, leaning over and speaking in a low voice. 'What happens to all the Egglos and Rowbots now that Hugh has had a dose of his own medicine?'

'Nothing,' replied Grandad. 'When the source of the messages is 'down,' nothing will be transmitted. The lights will still glow, but they won't have any effect. The schools have got a great product for free! Brian won't get his investment back unless they order more.'

'And he promised to supply unlimited books for the Rowbots for six months!' added Alice.

'Excellent, that'll hit him where it hurts most!' said Thomas. 'Right in the pocket!'

'Nothing more than he deserves,' declared Grandma. 'Brian and Hugh are rotten eggs! Do you think Hugh will go back to work?'

'Oh, I'm sure he will,' replied Thomas. 'He'll still want to make money. He just won't be able to harm people in the process. So he probably won't be much use to Brian any more.'

'How long do you think those drops will continue to have an effect on him?' asked Grandma.

'I've no idea,' admitted Thomas. 'I'm amazed they worked at all on him, really. If they start to wear off, Grandad will have to do a bit of dream travel and give him a top up.'

'Let's hope he sleeps with his mouth open, then!' said Grandad.

*

Grandad had read through the notebook Alice had found in Hugh's lab, and suggested that the person to give it to would be Nona. She would know exactly what to do with the information within it.

'Let me take it,' insisted Thomas. 'I need to visit her again, anyway.'

Nona seemed glad to see him. She didn't get many visitors and certainly wasn't expecting a gift. The notebook came as something of a shock; she sat down in her armchair and stared at it, transfixed. 'Where did you get this from?' she asked.

'Hugh Rowbottom's lab at the windmill,' he replied.

Nona raised her eyebrows. 'He has a lab? Well, I suppose I shouldn't be surprised. You know, I've suspected something for a while, when I heard about the nature of your abilities. Yours, Alice's and Hugh's, I mean. I realised that younger generations were evolving, and wondered if a local external influence was to blame. But I wasn't expecting this. This is a real blast from the past. I never thought we would learn to harness the mysterious forces of nature. This could have a great influence on my work!'

'Grandad thought you would make the best use of it,' explained Thomas with a grin.

'Well, I'm honoured, thank you,' said Nona, holding the notebook to her chest.

'Er, I did make a copy of it first.'

Nona smiled. 'I like your thinking. Which is one of the reasons I want to ask you something. Would you be interested in becoming my apprentice?'

Thomas was elated. 'I might consider it,' he replied, trying not to sound too eager.

'I already know that you're studying biochemistry. And I'm convinced that your abilities would bring great benefits to my magical engineering projects,' Nona continued. 'As well as to the village in general. You can heal without Finwips risking a visit to the hospital. X-rays are out of the question for us, as you know.'

Thomas nodded.

'And I can't begin to tell you how useful it would be to move components without actually touching the experiments.'

'Oh, I know what you mean,' said Thomas. 'I can only be here in the holidays, though. And even then, only some of the time. But I could do research while I'm at university and send it to you.'

'I was hoping you'd say that! Welcome aboard!' she declared, shaking his hand.

Thomas returned to the dining room looking rather smug, but before Alice could ask him why, Grandad asked them both to sit down and listen to what he had to tell them. Grandma obviously knew already – she looked less than impressed. He explained that after their conversation last weekend, he had spoken to Felix. Apparently, he gave his stone to Patrick before Hugh was born. When Hugh was small, he played with it all the time, he seemed to have a connection with it. Recently, Patrick gave it to him as a bit of a joke for his twenty-first birthday.

Thomas seemed confused. 'I thought Felix had nothing to do with them, how does he know Hugh has it?'

'Ah. This is where it gets interesting. He hadn't seen Hugh since he was a toddler. Then suddenly, he turned up on his doorstep in Devon last year, bearing gifts and that flamin' stone.'

'Oh great,' groaned Thomas. 'Couldn't Felix tell he was a Sinwip?'

'No, Hugh's too clever for that. It was just before his metamorphosis, but even before, he sensed something about that stone, and Patrick told him where it came from. Felix said Hugh seemed so nice, he was convinced he was going to be a Finwip like us. He told him everything about Arcanum Cove and let him stay for a couple of weeks.'

'No! Then what?' asked Alice.

'Felix was hurt and disappointed. Hugh came home one evening with more stones, then left that same night. He hasn't heard from him since.'

Alice was appalled. 'Did you tell him what Hugh really is?'

'I did, though I didn't need to. He already suspected, after he disappeared like that. It's very sad. The poor chap was over the moon, thinking he had another good grandchild like Jeremy's boys.'

'Oh dear,' said Alice quietly. 'And his grandaughter – Hugh's sister? What was she?'

'Finwip,' replied Grandad. 'His pride and joy. That really was a tragic accident.'

Alice felt awful now for encouraging Grandad to get in touch with his old friend. All it had done was confirm Felix's worst fear.

'Did you tell him that Lucinda and Isabella are good people?' asked Alice, hopefully.

'I didn't dare. There's still time for them to change.'

Alice was startled. For some reason it had never crossed her mind that Lucinda could become a Sinwip. Or even a Finwip – now that *would* be complicated. She didn't really know Isabella; she was at college studying fashion design.

'I'm wondering if Hugh's major grudge against Finwips stems from jealousy,' Grandad went on. 'Felix said Hugh was dreadfully jealous of his sister before she died, because he thought she was Patrick's favourite.'

'I'm sorry about all this,' mumbled Alice. 'What a mess.'

'Well, one good thing came out of it,' said Grandad. 'Felix has invited us to stay with him and his wife whenever we like! He's absolutely thrilled that you're both Finwips. And dead envious of your abilities!'

'What's his ability?' asked Thomas.

Grandad scratched his beard. 'Er ... let's make that a surprise for when you meet him, shall we?' There was plenty of protesting from Thomas and Alice, but he wouldn't budge.

'Another thing, Grandad,' began Alice, 'shouldn't you be wearing a different colour now you know what your real ability is? Yours is a rare gift now, not an artistic one.'

'Shh!' he snapped. 'Don't you dare say anything unless Imogen remembers! I like my regal gold robes – purple isn't my colour. Strong colours don't suit men of my age!'

'Even with your dream body?' asked Thomas. They all laughed, apart from Grandad, who always got rattled when people had a joke at his expense. Even Jack seemed to be laughing, though that might just be because he'd had so much food and attention from everyone in the village.

'Come on, we should make a move,' said Grandad. 'Your mum will go mad if we're late for dinner. I hope you're still hungry, your grandma has made a pudding.'

'Did someone mention Grandma's pudding?' asked Seb, who had noticed they were getting ready to leave. 'If it's another cheesecake, I'm inviting myself to dinner!'

'No, it's a ...'

'Don't tell him, Grandma!' interrupted Alice. 'He's had far too much sweet stuff already. Haven't you Seb?' she added, glaring at him.

'Ooh, that reminds me!' he replied, smiling to himself. 'You should have seen the puddings at the Windmill Restaurant! The food looked really good, you should try it. It's only ninety-five pounds for three courses.'

They all looked at each other and burst out laughing.

'Only?' said Alice. 'Oh, Seb, now we know what Hugh asked the green liquid to do!'

Seb turned red. 'Ninety-five pounds isn't at all expensive for ... oh, crikey. Yes it is! Aaargh! Wash my mouth out! Listen to me, recommending Rowbottom's restaurant! It really did look nice though, until I knew Hugh had done something to it.'

'And I smothered it in fire extinguisher foam!' added Grandad.

'Oh, Seb, what a shame you ate something there!' said Grandma sympathetically. 'It obviously worked on you, so we know you're not a Finwip yet.'

Seb smiled. He appreciated the '*yet.*'

'Thomas, we'll wait a few minutes before we leave for your house,' said Grandad. 'We don't want your parents to be suspicious if we all arrive together. Don't let it slip that we've seen each other already today.'

Alice sighed. She found it so difficult not to mention events in the village to her parents. She squeezed back into the lift with Jack, then they headed home. Thomas still looked very cheerful. 'What's put you in such a good mood?' she asked.

'Well, I don't like to brag ... but you're lucky enough to be related to the future 'Magic Engineer' of the village. I don't quite know how I'll fit it all in, though. I've got more books to read this holiday than you've read in your lifetime.'

'Bet I could read them quicker.'

'Don't rub it in! I can't believe I'm Nona's new assistant. I hope you're not jealous.'

'Not at all,' replied Alice with a smile. 'Imogen has already told me that I'll be *her* replacement. One day, Alice Parker will be head of Finwip village.'

Thomas didn't reply to that bombshell. But Alice could swear that Jack was smiling at him ...

*

Dinner was a success. Alice and Thomas pretended to greet their grandparents for the first time that day, and they all finished their food, though Grandma struggled.

'That was a delicious roast, Caroline,' said Grandad, patting his full stomach.

'I'm glad you enjoyed it,' she replied. 'I'm just sorry there were no peas. I was sure there was a bag in the freezer.'

Thomas looked down at the floor, trying not to laugh. Alice held her napkin over her mouth to hide her smile. Still, everything ran smoothly until Thomas announced that he was intending to change courses when he returned to uni. He had decided he would rather study medicine than biochemistry.

His father looked as though he was having heart failure at the table. 'What?' he croaked. 'What's brought this on? Don't get me wrong, I'm all in favour of medicine, but ... dear me, that's going to add another few years, isn't it?'

Thomas nodded. His mother patted his back; she approved of his decision. Alice and her grandparents smiled. They knew exactly what had prompted this.

'Just as I thought our finances were improving,' moaned his dad. 'No more take-aways during the week. It'll be one a month. And you'll have to get a job in the holidays, Thomas. We paramedics aren't as well paid as GPs! When you're a doctor, we shall expect slap-up meals and reservations in the best retirement homes! And we'll have to do without a holiday this year, I'm afraid.'

Thomas looked guilty now.

'Well, I couldn't take time off from the funeral parlour anyway,' said his mother. 'We're so busy since the competition closed down, I haven't organised more staff yet.'

'Actually, I hope to be a surgeon, not a GP,' Thomas clarified, trying to justify it. 'I just want a more rewarding career – I'd like to save lives.'

His mother frowned. 'Not too many,' she warned. 'Or you and your dad will put me out of business!'

'I might be able to organise a holiday for Alice and Thomas,' said Grandad. 'It wouldn't cost anything to stay with my old friend in Devon. In fact, he's already invited us.'

'I'm up for a free holiday!' said Thomas. Alice nodded enthusiastically.

'You could always stay with my parents in Florida,' replied their mother.

'Or my sister in Berlin,' suggested Grandma.

'Er, I don't fancy anywhere hot,' said Thomas, thinking about their wings. Heat wasn't good for them.

'And I'm not keen on flying,' added Alice, eager to meet Felix and visit Arcanum Cove.

Thomas snorted and tried to disguise it as a cough.

'That's settled then,' said Grandad with a satisfied grin. 'You'll enjoy it, I promise. I'll make sure it's a holiday to remember!'

Their father was very grateful. 'Are you sure you don't mind organising this dream trip, Dad?'

'Not at all. I've got a gift for that sort of thing.'

My Other Titles

Alice Parker's Metamorphosis

Alice Parker & The Secret of Arcanum Cove

Alice Parker & The Sound of the Silent

One Strange Christmas

If you would like to be informed when new titles are published, please email nicolapalmerwriter@gmail.com

About the Author

Nicola Palmer lives in Warwickshire, England. She likes animals, chocolate, vegetables and coffee. One day she hopes to grow wings and live in an underground village.

Unfortunately, Nicola doesn't have a magic letterbox, but she can be contacted at:

facebook.com/AliceParkersAdventures
twitter.com/nicolalpalmer
nicolapalmerwriter.blogspot.com

If you have enjoyed reading this book, we would love to hear from you. You can share your thoughts via one of the links above, or, if you purchased the book online, reviews can be posted on the vendor's website.

Thank you!

Printed in Great Britain
by Amazon

77166524R00081